PHILIP LEDERER

Margo

Copyright © 2023 by Philip Lederer

All rights reserved. No part of this publication may be reproduced, stored or transmitted in any form or by any means, electronic, mechanical, photocopying, recording, scanning, or otherwise without written permission from the publisher. It is illegal to copy this book, post it to a website, or distribute it by any other means without permission.

First edition

ISBN: 979-8-218-32619-7

This book was professionally typeset on Reedsy. Find out more at reedsy.com

For my family... dead and alive

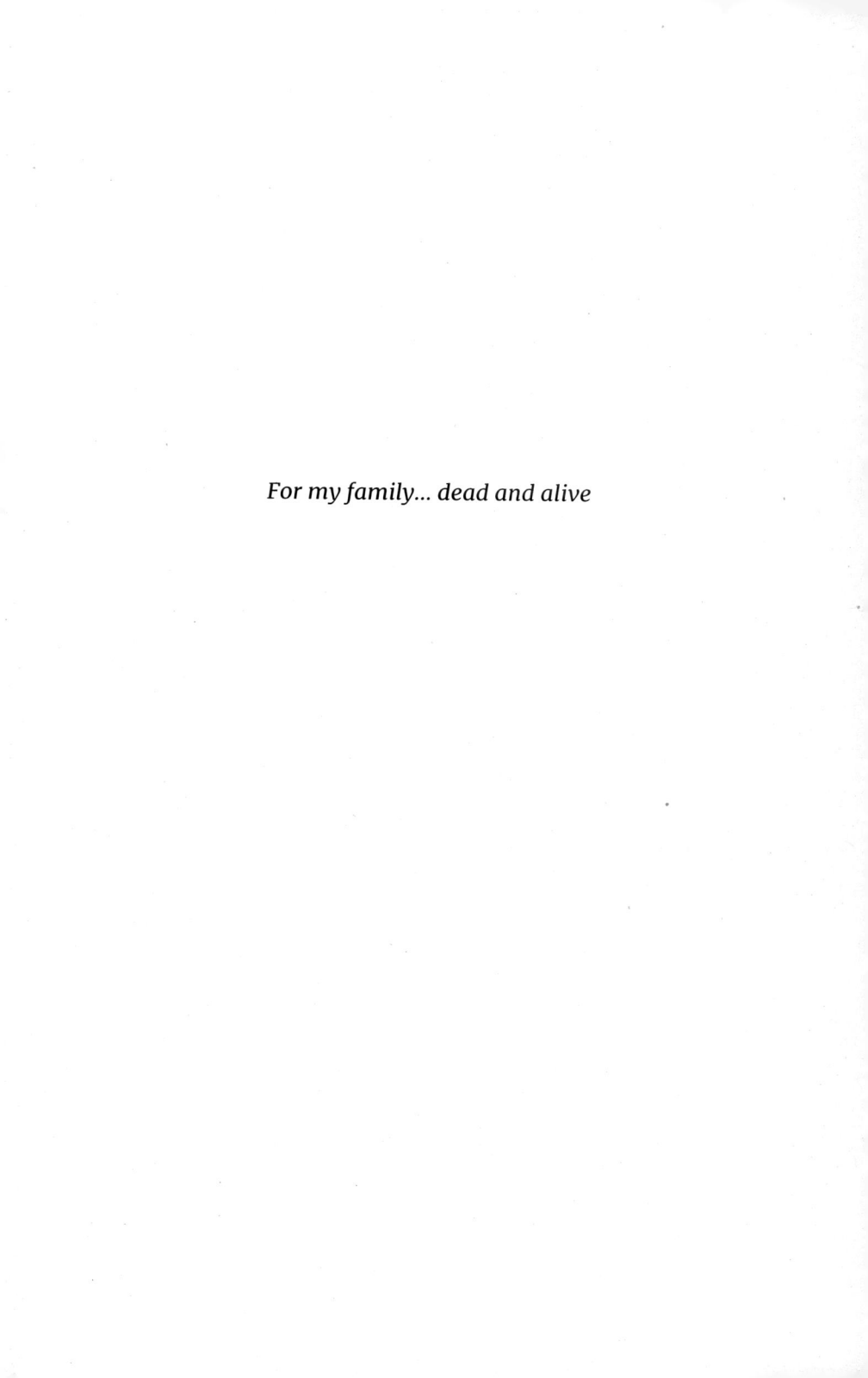

Foreword

This is my diary... a year in the life of a father, son, husband, dog lover.

It's mostly true, although a bit of fiction has crept in.

The names have been changed to protect the innocent and the guilty.

Let's get going.

Acknowledgement

I am particularly grateful to my wife, Kristen Lee; my son, Joseph Lederer; and my mother, Ann Lederer. Additional thanks to Keishon Graham, Damani Coates, Dan Ginotti, Gerard Robertson, Azeen Khan, Lauren Fisher, David Mischoulon, Janna Frelich, Muna Sheikh, Joel Wennerstrom, Murtuza Gunja, Ja-Yun Cho, Chad Ebesutani, Sam Wurzel, Gabriel Popkin, Adam Omar Hosein, Grier Merwin, Olga de la Calle, Rick Bird, Jose Viana, Lisa Moths-Rebrovic, Emily Lowenberg, Abby Rezendez, Betty Keller, Asad Nawaz, Peeyush Bhardwaj, Carol Toney, Phil Toney, Dhruv Kazi, Rusty Chandler, Josh Dankoff, Ben Sigelman, Yue Fang, Xiuhuan Yan, Michael Rhodes, Mary Lenihan, Bevin Kenney, Martin Balla, Kate Mitchell Balla, Ruvandhi Nathavitharana, Jim Tobias, Shin Ahn, Celso Khosa, Matt Crull, Ben Hulley, Susannah Graves, Ga-Young Lee, Hyun-Sik Yang, John Jewett, Colin Harris, Dan King, Brian Yablon, Adam Reich, Teresa Sharpe, Martha Ellen Katz, Andrew Gosselin, Carolyn Shadid Lewis, Matt O'Brien, Susan Racine, Vivek Naranbhai, Cristina Chang, Ghulam Khan, Seth Goldman, Megan Tan, Jurgens Peters, Anthony Prince, Marge Louisias, Sim Kimmel, Rob Flax, Eve Sorum, John Fulton, Emily Edwards, Stefan Lanfer, Peng Sun, Peter Downing, and Dan Janis, among many others. Also, gracias, of course, to Margo.

1

Post-Thanksgiving

November 27, Sunday, 7:02 AM

Well, we've been here before.

When I was ten, I wrote a mystery, "Choppers in Alaska," based on the Hardy Boys, with kidnappings and AK-47s. Never published.

When I was 32, I conducted interviews of clinicians at Maputo Central Hospital. I was hoping to compile them into a book—"A Right to Health: Medical Education in Mozambique." The manuscript was never published.

At 37, I wrote my first novel, "The Beltline," a dystopian 250 page thriller about a superbug, a deadly bacteria which sweeps the globe. I sent it to agents, but you get the idea.

Well, today, I decided this string of failures must end. So I set a "DDD" for myself—I'll publish my first book by December 31 of next year. I have ~13 months. That could mean getting accepted by a traditional publishing house or self-publishing. Somehow this manuscript has to come out!

And what's it about? Frankly I don't have any idea. It's fiction, nonfiction, memoir, diary, it has to be published!

I chomp into a piece of leftover Thanksgiving seitan. Chewy as steak, but with less cholesterol. The Beethoven violin concerto blasts on the stereo. I adjust my half marathon medal and keep working on the seitan (pronounced similarly to "Satan").

So why are you going to read my book? I can get my therapist and psychoanalyst to listen to my book, but I'm *paying* them.

Perhaps I will write funny prose, and you will be hooked—but with my track record...

Don't worry about the readers.

You might be wondering what a "DDD" is?

My father (Professor Albert Lederer, RIP), told me about this concept years ago.

A "Deadline" gets broken too frequently—but not a "Drop Dead Deadline." If you don't meet your DDD, you perish. So I have my marching orders, December 31 of next year.

November 28, Monday, 7:23 AM

So far so good—I'm writing. And Margo and I are walking up Calle Santa Rosa. Sunny and warm. "Hey," I say, and get her to turn around; we head toward the Little Free Library.

Last night was a disaster, but Kathy seems to have forgiven me. Our usual conflicts—food and screen time, and John was in the middle of both arguments.

We pass a house with its raised beds. Then Granola's home. Then Zoltan's old apartment. These walks remind me of the book, "Winesburgh, Ohio." Our neighborhood, its stories.

Margo is sniffing at a dead tomato plant.

I like my street. *Black Lives Matter* signs, *Stop Asian Hate* signs. It's progressive, as far as streets go. I wonder if we should schedule a winter holiday party. But after organizing the fall block party, I don't know.

2

Granola and Nellie come up the hill and I prevent Margo from playing, because of the viral papilloma on her mouth. "Cooties," Nellie says.

Down we go, past the Little Free Library; I put my books in. I feel good. On Day 1, I have written something. And I am going to publish this book.

DDD.

Back home, Margo is sniffing the ground and I'm pulling her past our SUV with its bumper sticker, "Help Farm Animals, Don't Eat them."

Margo races up the steps. We go back in the house, and Oma and John are measuring his height. "4 foot 5," he exclaims.

"Wow," I say. "Goodbye, have fun," to John.

"Have fun," to Kathy, kissing her.

"Have fun," to Wayharmoni.

"Have fun," to Margie-Pargie.

And John says, "*Don't have fun,*" to the dog.

I start walking my bike, thinking about how good my life is, and the silliness of last night's fight. So what if they wanted to get Indian food? So what if Oma let John read an ebook on her iPad and he called it "his" iPad.

It triggered my neuroses.

I go down a neighboring street, past the Scarecrow at #31. I put on The Chieftains "Bells of Dublin," pull my sock up, don my reflective yellow gloves.

November 29, Tuesday, 3:52 PM

So I was thinking about Malcolm X Health Center, where I work, and sadly, it feels like a sweatshop. A place where the main issue is profit, how many pieces of "clothing" you can make (how many patients you can see).

Everything at Malcolm X is driven by MEGA, the electronic medical record. It's about how quickly we can make a diagnosis, type in billing codes, and click through menus.

Malcolm X is located in Dorchester, Massachusetts. It's one of the poorest neighborhoods in Boston. Most of our patients are people of color — Cape Verdean, Dominican, Puerto Rican, African American...

November 30, Wednesday, 5:30 AM

I'm sipping my Brazilian coffee and eating toast. I review the text message I sent to colleagues at the union.

FYI—We have another issue to add to our demands—workplace safety at Malcolm X. It's complicated but several providers have had incidents when they have been threatened in the exam room. We asked the administration to change the rooms so the patient chair is by the window so the clinician has a better chance to escape if the patient is menacing. But so far no response...

Supposedly one reason they haven't reoriented the rooms is because the tile underneath the exam tables is gone, so new flooring would have to be installed. It comes down to money.

I remember March 2020, during COVID, when I pressed the administration at my previous job to provide us with better personal protective equipment. Not so successful. I'm determined to succeed at Malcolm X.

Ok, time to run. I'm happy it's 40 degrees. Ron is going to be there.

At 3 PM, on a telemedicine session with my therapist, Dr. Erin Beck

"... I have to see patients fast... and because I have my panel capped, and I have these problems with insurance companies like Blue Cross... and another company rescinded my credentialing — I see the patient and have to mark what their health insurance is..." I say.

"You're the one who has to pay attention to that?" she asks.

"Yeah."

"That's interesting—and frustrating..." she says.

"Yeah... and then this question... I guess Malcolm X backed off on firing me because they haven't really been pushing that the last couple months, but Dr. Roach does keep bringing up if they should keep my patient panel closed."

And then I tell her about a patient, 24-years-old, HIV positive, homeless, with a child... I shake my head.

After the session with Dr. Beck, I call to set up a dance class at Arthur Miller.

December 1, Thursday, 6:34 AM

Back from a run, and I'm thinking about the conversations we had bounding up and down Busey Hill. I told Joey about my DDD New Year's Resolution, and he confided in me his goal to do a 100 mile backpacking trip on a trail in northern New England next summer. (He also reported that he's a Taylor Swift fan).

Pablo is more soft spoken—his New Years Resolution might be cooking more chicken...Now Taylor Swift is on an NPR Tiny Desk Concert, "If I was a man,"—a song that Joey had recommended... I listen for a couple minutes, then put Charlie Parker on, "Out of Nowhere..."

I think about my grumpiness last night when Wayharmoni was throwing headers to John... I was enjoying it, but I did a bit of sabotaging. I don't mind soccer, but I don't want John to get in the habit of heading the ball... I believe it *might* lead to traumatic brain injury.

Just breathe...

I put on Christian Howes, jazz violinist with Les Paul, playing "The Days of Wine and Roses." And I realize today is December 1st, World AIDS Day.

December 2 Friday, 6:50 AM

I'm back from a run... it was good, 31 degrees, and we went 5 miles. I had some ideas—like a chess club at the the Arnold Arboretum School.

Or purchasing a "giant chess" set for John for Xmas? We don't have space for it inside, but it would be fun to play on the back porch.

Gary and I were talking about racquet sports—the pickle ball craze, badminton, and my favorite, ping pong. Because we had that when I was a kid, and Nanna even played.

I put on Christian Howes and loop it using the Youtube clip function. Margo sidles up to me and sniffs, licks, and rubs her whiskers against me....

So what of yesterday?

I had so much therapy—an hour of music/art therapy with Anna, focused on cleaning... a half hour with Dr. Park, talking about the same topic. So much time spent on cleanliness—what can I do to keep the bathroom clean, to not react against the idea of a "cleaning service?" Kathy isn't likely to change her beliefs, and neither will I...We don't want our home life to be like Guernica.

Anna and I talked about music therapy/arts—I would be interested in auditing a course at Lesley University if it were feasible. But for some reason, it isn't easy to do.

Anyway, she told me the story of a Venezuelan pianist and improviser named Gabriela Montero—a research study showed that improvisation is associated with activation of various brain domains.

So I'm on the right track in my jazz violin studies with Bob Parker.

But what of my DDD? I've been brainstorming about the authors I know—what do they have that I don't? Are they smarter than me? More focused? More well-connected? (Probably). I'm thinking of trying to speak to them—how they got agents, etc.

Another idea I had was to email Babe Cohen, my best friend from high school, a writer. Come to think of it, I'll email him right now.

December 3, Saturday 1:14 PM

It's raining and I'm drinking juice while listening to cellist Mike Block. John is still at Korean school, and Wayharmoni and Margo are in the kitchen. I look at my notes from this morning's run.

- Ron was telling me about the Tedeschi Trucks Band.
- Thank God for the Mobil gas station across from the BU campus, and its bathroom.
- Martin and Gary were talking about the Walnut Hills School, the crew/swimming teams, etc.
- I ran by a ghost bike in Brookline and took a closer look. RIP Bannon Williamson (1976-2016).
- I pass a labeled Northern Red Oak and think about this idea of educating the public about trees by marking them.
- I sit in a wooden chair on the Pinebank Promontory overlooking Jamaica Pond. The 5K race will begin soon, and I assume Lester will come—he said he would.
- Lester doesn't come.

- I see a recumbent bike go by and think about how I've been interested in recumbent tricycles.
- I finish 42nd in the 5K. I chat with the British ophthalmologist who researches retinitis pigmentosa. This time we talk about his daughter's chronic pain and also prevention of cardiovascular disease.
- Back at home, I eat the sweet potato Wayharmoni boiled for me and look at a couple of the books I picked up from the Little Free Library. I grab an audiobook (CDs), by Robert Gerzon—"Finding Serenity in the Age of Anxiety."
- I flip open this week's copy of the Bay State Banner—there is an interesting article about a Malcolm X opera.
- John and Oma return from Korean school and Tae Kwan Do and suddenly he's doing all these punches and kicks.

December 4, Sunday, 8:33 AM.
I tell Oma about my plan to resign from Malcolm X on December 31 of next year if we haven't unionized. "I can't stay in a dead end place for years upon years," I tell her.

Our new Christmas tree "smells so good," she says.

I rub Margo's snout.

I try to think about what I'd like to "Accomplish" today, so I can say "Mission Accomplished."

"Apa, that music is annoying, hearing it over and over," John calls to me. I have a Christian Howes clip of "The Days of Wine and Roses" looping, because I'm paying Bob Parker $75/violin lesson, and am I really making the progress I'd like? Similarly, I'm paying Dr. Fanon $125/psychoanalysis session, and am I making the psychological progress I'd like?

"Can I just listen 5 more times?" I negotiate...

Back to the DDD. Should I be writing to agents? Or just trying to write?

December 5, Monday 5:22 AM
I'm awake—last night there was some tossing and turning because of worries about the Boston Public Schools. We were at a friend's whiffle ball party, sitting around the fire pit, singing Bob Dylan songs, but sobering was that they pulled their son out of BPS. Sobering because we should be investing everything we have in our public schools, and BPS is hemorrhaging students. It reminds me of my dad, wanting John in a private school, and we acquiesced initially, but then changed our minds...

I ask myself, since I'm reading a Harriet Tubman biography, "What would Moses do?"

And then, at 8:28 AM
I'm in the urgent care provider room at Malcolm X wearing my white coat. I'm feeling a little relieved—just one more year in this prison—if we can't unionize by New Years of next year...

And then, at 5:12 PM
We're at the JP library. "I want to be a baseball expert," John says, reading one of his books... A white haired grandpa walks by—memories of my dad... how time passes quickly...

Also thinking about this Yale lawsuit I learned about, alleging discrimination against students struggling with mental health issues. I emailed it to my lawyers.

December 6, Tuesday, 11 AM
I meet with Dr. Jung from Physician Help Inc... she asks, "are things getting any better.... have you made any changes to your medications?"

I tell her that Dr. Basch made the decrease from 900 mg to 750 mg of lithium, and she asks, "have you noticed any difference?"

Umm...

"No, not really," I tell her. And she asks me how things are going at Malcolm X. I tell her about the same, "chaotic..." and talk to her about Dr. Humble's resignation, and his criticisms of the administration. She says that's "unfortunate... is it because of how they're treating the physicians?"

I tell her that "everything is multifactorial and there are layers of personality conflicts."

She asks how my mood is, and I tell her it's decent, despite the turmoil. Dr. Jung queries if there's anything "we can do for you?" and I answer, "within your power?"

I tell her I did the drug test which was negative; the neurology appointment is scheduled.

"Do you feel like the change in medication has helped with the ability to focus on your notes?" she asks. My notes—I answer that "I like to be scientific about things, and I can't put a number on anything related to my notes, so I take the 5th amendment."

She laughs. She asks, "are there any complaints about not responding to patient requests through MEGA?"

None.

"As far as I know, Dr. Trump and Dr. Roach were hoping things were going to improve for you, so I'm interested if they have anything to say. If there's anything you think would make a difference, is there anything that would be playing into your ability to fulfill their requests—to see more patients, write your notes?"

Am I stressed? At times, when the clinic gets busy—we have lost medical assistants, and hired new ones who aren't experienced. I tell her I feel like I'm under a "very intense lens, in part because of my history, because I am on the probation agreement... there's a level of how I'm being scrutinized because of the reports to Physician Help Inc."

She changes the subject.

It's all resting on me petitioning the medical board to end the probation agreement, but I need supportive letters from Malcolm X.

A Catch 22, it is. I can't petition the board because my Drs. Trump/Roach won't write a supportive letter. They won't write me a letter because I remain under this vigilant lens.

December 11, Sunday 6:23 AM

I'm sitting on the couch looking at the Christmas tree, and adjust my Santa hat—its pom fell down. My father used to wear a similar hat, even though he was Jewish—I suspect it reminded him of his father, Lewis "Red Lederer, who wore a Santa outfit to Cincinnati orphanages.

I stop writing on my legal pad. "Growth mindset," Dr. Phil, I tell myself. Yesterday after finishing the Tubman biography ("keep going" was her motto) I started a book by Carol S. Dweck PhD. Many people live in a "fixed mindset," but by embracing the possibility for change, we can develop our abilities.

So here I am—193.6 pounds of me. I'm aiming to get below 190 by New Years but unless I start fasting, that seems unlikely. I am building endurance despite not losing weight. My 5K time, half marathon time, and weightlifting testify to that. So even though I might be a little grumpy this morning, I should get dressed and jog.

I put my feet on Margo to try to warm them up. Holiday cards are another goal—I plan to mail at least 100 to family and friends around the country. Old school—the world might be spinning madly, to quote the Phil Ochs song, "Changes," but as long as I can put pen to paper, things are ok.

I see the light of dawn (blue) past the Xmas tree. I'm "Dr. Phil," leaving my troubles behind. I'll achieve my DDD...

December 12, Monday 6:45 AM

Another beautiful day in Purgatory," I tell Ron. He laughs. "Purgatory? Whaddya mean?" I try to explain, an indeterminate state, not heaven nor hell.

Ron says, "You know, if you do a run like this alone, you're miserable. And people might call you crazy. But if you do it with other people, it's fun!" We part ways, and I head home.

This morning, when I read the Boston Globe, I'm going to look for the most hopeful story I can find—it might be an obituary, or an article about someone overcoming adversity... a treasure hunt for one positive story.

December 13, Tuesday 6:39 AM

"Hazelnut coffee. The song, 'How High the Moon.' Ghostwriters for Bill Clinton, James Patterson, Phil Knight, Andre Agassi." I sit, shirtless, on the couch.

Of all the themes Ron and I discussed today, the most actionable seems like the idea of a ghostwriter.

My friend Babe suggested I go after agents. But don't I need a book to hook an agent?

My writing better be good—"Catch-22" or "Confederacy of Dunces" or "House of God" funny, James Patterson page turner, Anne Frank pathos, etc. The other idea is to make a list of physician-writers and ask for help:

- Samuel Shem
- Abraham Verghese

- Danielle Ofri
- Atul Gawande
- Louise Aronson
- Mark Vonnegut

Suddenly, Margo and John have joined me on the couch, the dog is licking me, and John has his baseball card binder. Oma comes into the living room, and I tell them my plans. "It's a comedy," I say.

"You have too much comedy stuff," John retorts.

December 14, Wednesday, 6:56 AM

It was an arctic run this morning to Larz and I spent most of it talking about a subject I usually scorn—*robotics*. I am a luddite, a ecosocialist / artist praising music, trees, gardens, and oceans over technology and sprawl. The automation of everything gets me angry.

But this morning Gary was upset because our kids' school is falling behind. He would like an after school robotics club—and as much as I'm leery of STEM, I thought it was a decent idea, as long as kids aren't learning to pilot military drones. I told him I'd email Julie Shah, an MIT robotics professor I knew years ago.

So maybe I'll be the president of the Arnold Arboretum School Robotics Club, despite my reluctance.... What else?

We were talking about summer camps and I was praising the Wheelock Theatre Program. I'd like John to have an artistic endeavor, and it could be acting, dance, or visual arts. Wheelock might be a good way to explore those disciplines.

Then at 2:00 PM

I'm waiting for a Zoom with my Man's Greatest Hospital nutritionist, Fats, to begin. What can I say? My weight is 193, but

I'm running and trying to eat healthily. Feeding Margo makes me remember how we got her to lose weight—we fed her less...

I tell Fats a New Year's Resolution, to get better at salads. And, I will cook stir-fry with veggies, or bean soups, but as far as having salad skills, I'm not great. We talk about being healthy at every size and getting rid of weight stigma which is a good conversation to have...

December 15, Thursday 6:40 AM

I finally caught up to the "small butts" at the end of our 4 mile run this morning. Let me explain.

I was chubby growing up, and have always had body image issues. During high school I lost weight and enjoyed being a member of the cross country and track teams. But in my adult life my weight has yo-yo'd. I have a belief that if I was lighter my running would be easier. I'm not trying to get back to my high school weight of 145, but it's impossible to not compare myself to the runners around me.

This morning it was Ron, Gary, Mary, and Rachel. All are svelte in their spandex, while I was wearing baggy sweatpants and a ratty UC San Diego Medicine sweatshirt. And more importantly—I couldn't keep up.

The majority of the run I was 30 feet behind, alone in the dark, chasing their headlamps. True, my body is 30+ pounds heavier than theirs. But yesterday's talk with Fats helps me see that's ok, and I can change my habits. In the end, I finally caught up to the others.

Yours, Phil

PS—I'm still working on developing a growth mindset. Just like Michael Jordan was cut from his high school basketball team, the challenges I've had to overcome are making me focus. The "synthesis" word of the week from Dr. Fanon's psychoanalysis session was "Band," as it takes a "Band" of brothers and sisters to achieve our dreams.

December 16, Friday 6:42 AM

I'm sitting on the couch listening to Sonny Rollins playing "How High the Moon." The dog licks the pillow and the wind whistles. Next to me rests a new book I picked up, "Life Strategies—Doing what works, doing what matters," by Phillip C. McGraw PhD (AKA 'Dr. Phil'). I look at his face on the cover. Unbelievable. I've known about him for years and have been compared to him—"Hey Dr. Phil!"

Right now I'm trying to use "Life Strategies" as motivation. If a guy like Dr. Phil McGraw can publish a book, certainly Dr. Philip A. Lederer can do the same. I inscribe McGraw's book—I'll carry around "Life Strategies" until I have published mine. DDD.

Yours, Dr. Phil

And 2:47 PM

Pat the plumber just left after fixing our radiator. I also talked to Terry on the phone and then fooled Aaron by text message, telling him Terry was going to "prison." True, but it was just to moonlight as a doctor overnight. Terry is ok; Aaron was laughing.

I turn off my phone—crazy stuff happens on Fridays; I don't want to hear it. Margo settles next to me. I consider my options—phoning my mother's doctor's office to make sure her TSH can be drawn; practicing the trumpet or violin before Kathy / John get home; working on MEGA; masturbation (!).

Or writing.

I remember John telling me that in the Japanese baseball

league, they throw spitballs. So if they are used to spitballs in the Japanese ballparks, they will do well in the MLB. The new Red Sox player had 21 homers in Japan and should hit more than that here. (We only throw spitballs at Malcolm X).

The hissing of the radiators, the rumble of the Orange Line. And Pat the Plumber—he told me of his divorce, his 2 kids with their mom.

Joan Baez on our record player, her *Noel* album, "Angels we have Heard on High."

December 17, Saturday 5:53 AM

It's like Groundhog Day—I'm on the couch, looking at the tree, listening to Sonny Rollins. But today I want to talk about trauma.

It was 1984 and I was on the playground at Carnegie Mellon Preschool, walking on the railroad ties.

The memories are flashes of light. My father driving me to Shady Side Hospital; later on, the smell of anesthesia. And the scar on my top lip. Everything was well; the surgeon had cleaned out the wood-chips. Everything was well except for three things.

First, I have a hypothesis that my fall was a trauma that led to a lifetime of anxiety. Hard to know. Second, I've always been musical, and love whistling—and am reasonably good at it, but my lips are slightly asymmetrical. The scar is apparent every time I puff out my cheeks.

Third, Rochester Hills, Michigan, 6th grade, early 1990s. There was no school orchestra so I couldn't play violin, but there was a band. My father had played sax in high school, but for some reason I became a trumpeter. I learned to play, but I had a problem—my scar led to an asymmetrical embouchure. I had trouble hitting the high notes.

When we moved to Kentucky I went back to violin.

That would be the end of the story, except it isn't.

In 2018, I became distressed ("manic," the doctor said). I had purchased a trumpet at the woodwinds store next to New England Conservatory. I stood on the street corner and "busked"—I didn't get any money but I did speak with a woman named Randy Karr and her boyfriend. It turned out she had a business advising people on posture—she was a former ballerina. So a few weeks later I found myself in her studio learning to carry myself better.

But even now, the story isn't over, because recently I went back to my trumpet practice (at home, alone). There is something meditative about it; it's all about breathing. And with every note I have to reckon with my trauma.

I can play a chromatic scale, and I wonder if I practiced regularly if I could get decent at it.

The problem is Kathy doesn't like the trumpet.

But even now, the story isn't over—there is a certain intersectionality between trumpet and violin; one uses breath, mouth, and three fingers; the other arms, hands, a bow and strings.

And finally, there is a curious violin-like instrument which projects its sound through the trumpet bell, a "Stroh violin."

So that's the end of this wandering story.

December 18, Sunday 4:30 PM

I was vomiting this morning—a virus. Now I pick up a book by a lady named Linda Georgian "of the psychic friends network" entitled "Communicating with the Dead—Reaching Friends and Loved Ones Who have Passed on to Another Dimension of Life."

I look up at our triple decker and see Dan Truman and his girlfriend, 3rd floor—interesting how we are strangers even though we have lived in the same house for years. It's like Rear

Window.

My fingers get cold, so we walk back up Santa Rosa and Chuck comes down the front porch steps. He says how long the nights are this time of year, and I mention how things will turn around in a couple of days.

He agrees. "It's darkest before the dawn."

Inside, Oma and John are home after the stunning Argentina soccer victory, but she is upset. John was playing with Fidel for hours.

I show her Linda's book and ask if she wants to communicate with the dead. "Why not communicate with the living?" Kathy queries. Good point.

After some dreidel, played with peanuts and the first night of Hanukkah prayers from my grandmother's prayerbook, and some Itzhak Perlman music (the klezmer album 'In the Fiddler's House'), I'm alone with the menorah and tree. I flip through the Isaac Bashevis Singer book, "The Power of Light."

December 19, Monday 6:46 AM

Back from my run, where Suz was telling me of an organization called Oakland Reach, dedicated to lifting up public schools. Perhaps they could serve as a model for Boston.

Ron and I chatted about my upcoming marathon in Providence. We also talked about if I might be able to run the Huntington Beach Marathon when we are in LA, but I'm not clear on the dates. In addition, we traded utopian/dystopian novels—mine was "The Ministry for the Future," when LA floods due to climate change; his, Bill McKibben's, where Vermont brewmakers have to band together.

Joey told me his story of being on jury duty. The man on trial had been convicted of a sexual crime years ago; his sentence was completed but then he was committed; he still seemed to present a danger to society.

I thought of my dad, his imprisonment for hashish, and his expungement, and my own situation with the medical board.

Just an hour ago I was emailing Van to see if we could speak to discuss petitioning the board, but this conversation with Joey gives me pause. The jury declined to release Joey's prisoner after his sentence and commitment. What would make the medical board end my admonishment, especially in the context of negative evaluations from Drs. Trump / Roach?

I suppose I could ask others at Malcolm X to write me letters of support, but would they?

December 20, Tuesday 7:00 AM

"I was chased by coyotes," I tell Pablo and Ron after I finally catch up to them.

They smile, then take off—and I'm left alone in Franklin Park. I'm slow, and mostly I'm rehashing yesterday's conversation with Angel, a nurse practitioner and member of Malcolm X management. She said that we have problems at the health center, but from her perspective, things are better than they've been.

Stories matter, and the question is if our narrative can punch through management's spin? What are the most successful organizing campaigns and how can we emulate them? The Montgomery Bus Boycott? The California farmworkers? What stories did those folks tell each other which gave them courage?

And 2 PM, Windy, Sunny

I'm standing outside Malcolm X, thinking about my talk with Elana Sawyer, head of HR. What can I say—I didn't want to throw Dr. Jesús Trump or Dr. Jo Roach under the bus, because although she says it's confidential, it can get back to them fast.

Elana does seem good hearted and wants things to be more supportive. It was helpful—me realizing the "Performance Improvement Plan" is a major stressor. Or the exam room safety, or the lack of an annual review. And the thing about Dr. Trump calling my cell phone about Maria being poorly treated? These are things that should be investigated.

Elana kept it close to the vest, however.

The other thing is, Dr Trump is not the problem. Dr Roach is not the problem.

They are *part* of the problem, in that they manage in an autocratic style. But we are the problem, we the people who have accepted this system of being exploited.

Elana might be friendly, but then at the end of our meeting she's talking about random things like telemedicine.

I don't think systemic change comes from talking to HR—except, in that, you have to look at yourself, and the work you are doing; think, why we're not doing more, why we're not on the streets, working with the Boston Public Health Commission?

December 21, Wednesday, 6:50 AM

I finally did it.

I emailed Shaquille, coordinator of the Youth Center, to see if Danny and I could volunteer.

Kathy and I moved to JP in March 2018, not thinking much about the Boston Housing Authority development (projects) a block away from our home. We were focused on the Arboretum, Jamaica Pond, etc. But little by little, we became aware of the development, where almost all residents are black and brown. (On Santa Rosa, most people are white).

When John was 5, we would play on the development's

playground. But gradually we started staying away. One reason might have been the shooting...

There are some links between the Santa Rosa and the development. We know the lady who walks her dog nearby. And Juan, an older man who parks his car on our street, putting cones in front/behind it.

And we have participated in the Youth Center's 5K fundraiser run. But the reality is, I haven't done anything for/with folks who live in the BHA development.

Part of that is being busy. But part of it is has to do with my own racism/fear. Do I *really* want to try to get involved with this youth center?

Just yesterday, Dr. Fanon and I agreed on my focus on being more "Zennish" next year—does taking on even more activities lead me to a Zen state?

Perhaps.

I'm not trying to be a white savior for these kids.

I'm just trying to see if Danny and I could help out.

3:00 PM

I'm sitting at Kathy's desk, joining the zoom with Dr. Bausch.

"How's the holiday season going?" he asks.

"Good. We're trying to figure out travel plans with this blizzard," I tell him. "We were going to drive to Ohio, but we might not."

We chat about Physician Help Inc, the medical board, and the lithium.

And he says, "the real test will be what Dr. Roach and Dr. Trump think of your work, so my hope is these issues they are concerned about will end.

December 22, Thursday, 6:57 AM

Margo is snuffling around my boots as I'm trying to warm up, while thinking about Manuel, a poor guy from Cape Verde, his job as a custodian on the line. I discussed it on the run with Pablo, and he said Manuel could call an attorney for mediation.

It also made me think about my own case in 2020. I could've filed an EEOC complaint but I didn't. And now with all the problems at Malcolm X I wonder if calling the government could help us?

I think we need to take a more pugilistic approach, reckoning back to my friend Marcus Williams, a civil rights attorney in DC. The system is broken, but we have to keep fighting, is his attitude.

Later, 5:16 PM

At clinic. The custodian walks by, busy but friendly. Works two jobs. I always feel guilty when I see him (low salary). I stand up and wander the health center. Happy holidays to the nurses. Candy is hoping for a sleet day tomorrow, she says.

I go into Dr. Humble's old office, and there are several ID's from 20 years ago on the desk. And a cup, with photos of the internal medicine residents and Jo Roach. I feel sad.

December 23, Friday, 6:33 PM

It's the Sixth night of Hanukah—we're watching the candles. Bambi's footsteps are pounding overhead; she's 3 years old now. I'm eating tofu and latkes and apple sauce, and reading Isaac Bashevis Singer. And I'm thinking of Pete, drowned while on a cruise.

I met him at least once—he conducted the orchestra the summer before last on a baseball field. I whistle Mozart's Eine Kleine Nachtmusik. Pete was my age.

I have my DDD, but this existence is so brief, like a Hanukah candle. Our lives spark, they burn. And what did we "Accomplish?"

"Ta mogo so?" Kathy asks in Korean. "Was it good?"

"Delicious," I say.

December 24, Saturday, 6 PM

Grandma is washing dishes. Margo wanders in. John enters, "I want to show you something," he says.

"Thanks for doing those," I tell my mother.

"Sure…. that music is very nice," she says, as we listen to "In My Solitude," Ella Fitzgerald.

Oma comes in.

The audio track switches to a sermon from the civil rights movement, and then, a spiritual, "Woke Up this Morning with my Eyes on Freedom;" we sang that in 2018 in the Poor People's Campaign.

We'll Zoom with the Toledo-ones later. Right now it's quiet—me, the candles, the jazz guitar on the speaker, probably Joe Pass…

I count the candles for tomorrow, the 8th night…. we have enough… I listen to the sound of my mom brushing her teeth after dinner—she is meticulous… I take off my Cape Cod Marathon medal… now Youtube Music switches its mix to Phil Ochs, folk singer… "When I've got somethin' to say sir, I'm gonna say it now…"

The candles are buds of wax and wick. I spin a dreidel—Gimel… the 3rd candle burned out. I know Hanukah is far from an important holiday in Judaism, but for me it's calming, connecting me to my ancestors.

December 25, Sunday, 6:50 AM

By the tree—listening to a recording of a Christmas Eve Sermon, the Reverend Dr. William Barber II, calling for a ceasefire in Ukraine. "As Gandhi once said, an eye for an eye makes the world blind..."

Oma drops dog kittles at Margo.

John grunts, stacks the presents on the couch, runs back and forth. "Oma come."

He opens one of the packages.

"Margo," I call, trying to get her over to us.

"Does she have a beard?" Grandma asks.

"It's a papilloma—a wart," I say.

The gifts: for John, a teenage mutant ninja turtles helicopter, from Grandma. Baseballs from Oma/me. A scarf for Grandma, knitted by Oma. A couple books for Oma... Drawings of rainbows John made.... I lock Margo in the bathroom so John can launch his drone.... it bounces across the living room ceiling. The music changes, "The Rebel Jesus," The Chieftains.

Grandma says she's going to the bathroom, then will make bread.

Kathy starts laughing—"I thought you said you are going to make bread in the bathroom."

December 28, Wednesday, 8:09 PM

I'm on the couch; Joan Baez is on the record player; Oma and John are at the dining room table playing a game. I think about Claude Fredericks, the Bennington professor described in an article in the New Yorker—his diaries are archived in the Getty. Mine are on legal pads on my bookshelf, and I'm hoping to turn them into a book. DDD.

I blow my nose and Margo raises her head; I pick up the little Phillips Audio Recorder on a lanyard around my neck.

"Blammo"—that's the game Kathy and John are playing.

December 29, Thursday, 5:58 AM

Zen and the Art of Motorcycle Maintenance. That book came to me overnight.

December 31, Saturday, 5:22 AM

On the toilet, writing on my yellow legal pad, thinking about my 6:45 AM run. The weather looks good. I just need to cut my toenails, and apply some Glide so I don't get blisters. And I want to carry some tissues with this cold. Also, I need to figure out the water situation—probably I should bring a bottle.

2

New Year

January 2, Monday 5:49 AM

The New Year is 1 day old; so far so good. I have my DDD, twelve months to go; we ate sauerkraut with fake hot dogs and potatoes with my mom for good luck. With the warm weather John and I enjoyed a pickup soccer game—kids and adults, and my son even played goalkeeper.

It doesn't seem like we have a group run this morning so I'll go a little later—maybe 6:45 AM with the sunrise.

What else?

I talked to Dr. Daneeka on the phone yesterday for about 20 minutes in anticipation of my meeting with Bridget Wilson, the Malcolm X Board chair. Gerald is always reconciliatory. Anyway...

The most interesting thing I appreciated from the phone call is the complex racial, class, educational, and gender issues at play at Malcolm X. For example, Bridget Wilson is Irish-American, and working class, and as a woman going up against more well-educated (theoretically) male doctors, there has been conflict over the years. And then, the racial elephant in the living room—

she (and most of the doctors) are white, and the majority of Malcolm X patients and staff are black/ brown.

Anyway, I suspect the health center is hanging on by a thread—it could easily be gobbled up by Man's Greatest Hospital, BMC, or Tufts Medical Center—and it's surprising it hasn't been.

Jacob Kahn told me Dr. Humble was the main reason it didn't happen before... and now George is gone.

So how will we unionize Malcolm X? Text messages won't hurt, but it's going to take face to face conversations, Bob Moses style.

–

Let's talk about an uncomfortable topic—sex and desire in marriage. Something seemed to change between Kathy and me the past year or so—the sex is still there, and good, but the desire level has dropped. Not easy.

(The other layer of complexity is my hyper-sexuality during my manic episodes freaked out Kathy).

What else?

My mother's moods remain a sore point. On Saturday I tried to convince her to let me program our new landline phone number into her Google Voice—but she became overwhelmed by having to learn something new.

8:04 PM

I'm thinking of what I want to say to Dr. William Locke, the former Chief Medical Officer for the Department of Defense, now at an academic medical center in the Midwest. Basically that patient safety is my priority along with delivering high quality medical care. However, I think the medical board's actions against my license are stigmatizing. What can I do?

Maybe Dr. Locke can help.

Van, my lawyer, hopes to petition the board but I feel pessimistic they will remove the restrictions. I'll tell Dr. Locke this what I consider due to workplace stress, i.e. an occupational health condition. What will he say?

But back to the moment—John is telling me about Auburn and Ole Miss baseball. This kid is a fanatic.

January 3, Tuesday 10:09 AM

I'm in my son's room, listening to jazz as he plays with baseball cards. I think of my indoor track workout this morning in Roxbury, the runners dancing to the hip-hop music between 200m laps.

"Apa, who are you going to send in to pitch?" John asks, bringing me back to the present.

Yes, the dilemma of modern life—Kathy and I stay together for us, for our kid, the 8-year-old, while we try to reconcile.

We can't stop aging—even with marathons and workouts at Mike's Fitness. And sexual excitement might not be the same as when we first met.

As my friend "Banjo Ben" says, people "accumulate baggage as they get older." Marriages accumulate baggage too—and a relationship might feel like a Chevy Chase movie.

-

I'm frustrated after my meeting with Bridget—the solution to the problems at Malcolm X Health Center is not to fire Dr. Trump. That will lead to more turmoil—I'm tempted to resign.

And then there's MEGA! Our EMR, which is terrible, the loads of messages piling up, and the neurosyphilis (?) patient from last week who is refusing lumbar puncture. I'm going to read the penicillin allergy article on Uptodate now.

8:03 PM

In bed. I'm trying to let go of the unpleasant meeting with Drs.

Trump and Roach—more gaslighting is how I felt.

At least there was nice salad with Oma/John, some looping ("Have you met Ms. Jones"). And I called Emilio—he texted me the classical guitar song he's working on.

Plus I talked to Rodrigo from the union. We need a meeting—maybe next Monday.

January 4, Wednesday 5:12 AM

I'm listening to Chet Baker play "Have you met Miss Jones?" His articulations are impressive, and when he "double times" it and plays sixteenth notes, it blows me away.

I take a sip of my coffee and think about the email I received from Jessie Texeira, a doctor who also has a diagnosis of bipolar disorder. I had sent a message to her and several others proposing a Zoom to discuss bipolar scientific research, particularly on treatment regimens and the role of the National Institute of Mental Health. NIMH has neglected to support clinical trials, instead focusing on basic science mechanisms.

I had been thinking about the role of ACT UP in pressuring the FDA and NIH to do more clinical research during the early days of AIDS, popularized in the book and movie "How to Survive a Plague." Why am I taking an antipsychotic, aripiprazole, which causes weight gain and diabetes, and provides an uncertain benefit, and lithium, which affects the kidneys and thyroid? I want better treatments. But the only way that this will *ever* occur is if affected patients advocate together and force the government to fund clinical research.

January 5, Thursday, 6:42 AM

Margo is sniffing at my knees, her whiskers rubbing against me, and John leans against me as well as he reads the sports page. I reminisce back to 2000, my trip to Israel, floating in the Dead Sea, covering ourselves with mud; hiking on the cliffs at Masada. Margo whines, climbs on the couch—I'm sandwiched.

On the Israel trip I rode a camel in the desert in a Beduin community. I connected with several other students and we created the Brown University "Jew Over 2, the Half-Jew Crew" when we returned to Providence. We organized a conference on the subject of children of intermarriage. To this day, I have identified as half-Jewish, a category which technically doesn't exist, and I've been crossing borders ever since.

And my son is half-Korean.

I long for community and belonging, but I also identify with the Groucho Marx joke, that I don't want to be a part of a club which would accept me as a member.

11:30 AM

In the primary care workroom, Maria is talking about our skinny security guards—"how are they going to stop somebody with a gun?" she asks. And she tells me the story of one of our nurse practitioners who was chased from room to room at Malcolm X by a patient.

We need to unionize.

Meanwhile, the administration wants us to fill out an "incident report" anytime anything happens. Why don't you fill out the incident report, Dr. Roach?

Nothing is simple, even getting a patient from the urgent care over to the podiatry clinic to be evaluated. The patient is an immigrant who only speaks Haitian Creole, and feels intimidated by going to the hospital.

Later, I see a man from Cape Verde who lived in Angola for years—my new favorite patient. "Hepa," he says, using the same expression that they use in Mozambique. He was in Luanda during the civil war.

I talk to Helder and Marquita—we need to unionize, I say.

We need metal detectors, better salary. And Marquita tells me about her son, who has autism and benefits from music therapy. Everything sensory, with drums, etc, is good for him. I'm so lucky John is healthy.

I bike over to the Community Center, an old building Malcolm X owns. I make my way into Bridget Wilson's inner sanctum.

"How are you?" I ask.

"My daughter just called, bitching at me because she sent two requests in MEGA to Tammy Smith asking if she could have her COVID booster because she's a teacher. And she has three to five year olds who think masks are what you wipe your nose on. She's luckily had COVID once, the last day of school... it was a miracle. She spent the next two weeks moaning about how they would have to pay her for that time off if she had gotten it during the school year."

She laughs. "Literally, the last day of school she came down with it. So she sent Tammy a couple of messages and the nurse called this morning to tell her to check the CDC guidelines."

"Hmm," I say.

"So can she get another vaccine? That one four months ago was her 4th."

I rack my brain, thinking about the data behind mRNA boosters and nod, somewhat hesitantly.

"She is immune compromised... she's a mess, but she's a joy... ok I'll tell her.... She's just mad she didn't get her question answered."

"Well Tammy Smith announced her resignation this morning," I said.

"What?"

"She announced her resignation."

"I'm hoping that will change," Bridget replied.

A long pause between us.

"I know she's overwhelmed," she said, "and I know why, and you know why, and we all know why..."

"Yeah..." I say softly.... Another pause. "So the reason I wanted to come back is I talked with Dr. Daneeka and several other providers, and I wanted to understand a little bit more. So, what it sounded like you were saying is you are planning to fire Dr. Trump. And I'm just wondering... it's a little bit complicated, but so much stuff has happened, so much stuff we don't like. For various reasons... it's complex... is there any other option, like reassign him..."

"Do you see Dr. Trump taking a lesser job?"

"Probably not."

"No," she said. "I mean it would be nice if we could think that way, and you didn't hear it from me that we're going to fire him, but I know the level of toxicity you people have been dealing with is just... we've heard it from everybody."

"Yeah," I say.

"That's no way... you shouldn't have to come to work every day and feel like... you have your patients who present problems to you that you have to solve. But that the people you are working for are part of the problem... that's not ok... You should be treated like human beings! I mean, I'm guessing because I don't know what Naren's plans are, I'm thinking Trump will be offered that, but... what are your thoughts on his little minion there?"

I look at her, confused.

"Dr. Roach," she explains.

"She's got a lot of nice qualities," I hem and haw. "We each have our quirks, our qualities that can be not so nice.... I think we want to take everybody and grow them somehow... it's idealistic."

"Right," she says. "I would hope that Naren is going to present Roach with... 'these are the things I have heard... if I continue to hear them, say goodbye.' Because she's become part of the problem too, from my understanding.... That's not ok... she's somebody you could say, 'would you take a lesser role.' But I don't see Dr. Trump doing that... I have heard people say that the only reason Trump wanted this job was so he could get back at Dr. Humble... Because years ago, the health center made a decision to go to a family practice model. And Trump was one of the docs who was let go. I can't imagine he spent 20 years angry about it, but maybe he did... And this is too bad, because not only did we lose Dr. Humble, but the other doctor who was going to join us is headed to Norton Street Health Center."

"Dr. Braider," I say, nodding.

"You've got some team-building to do."

"Big time... this morning when Tammy announced her resignation..."

"Did she cry?" Bridget interjects.

"She was on the video, so you couldn't really tell, but everyone's heads drooped. Because everyone loves her."

"Oh, when my daughter finds out, I'm in for a world of hurt. Because my daughter sees her.... I see her... I'm hopeful that we will be able to keep her. I'm hopeful.... I have no reason to be, but I'm the kind of person who is always maintaining hope... and I think we can make things change. I do. I think we have to make things change."

-

I send a text to our group of providers saying that if we can't have a safe health center, and if the bosses dismiss Maria's demand for metal detectors, we should go on strike.

January 6, Friday 6:51 AM

I'm walking by the BHA development thinking about Maria's passion for metal detectors. I asked Kristopher, my cousin, a police officer in another state, his thoughts. It's a sad world we live in where this is a concern—guns in clinics. I'm sort of learning, though, about advocating around issues—the medical assistants, we could write a petition and rally with them.

This you could almost rally around it—safety in the workplace.

I even remember the metal detectors at the medical board when I had to go there in 2018—they don't want guns in there. I was wearing my grey suit, and Van was next to me, and I had to take my cell phone out of my pocket, get wanded down.

I walk past Papercuts Book Shop—I so badly want my book to be in that bookstore.

I come up on the Little Free Library—that's kind of where you don't want your book to be. On the one hand, it means someone didn't like your book and threw it out. On the other hand, it means enough copies of your book were printed that they are still floating around.

And on the other side of South Street is the public library, a place you want your book to be.

So what is this all about—being recognized, acknowledged as intelligent, when you are someone living with a diagnosis of bipolar, marginalized, my medical license in jeopardy, my board certification revoked, a subpar score on neuropsychological testing—a kind of a Redemption Song.

Atop Busey Hill, I see the Massachusetts Department of Public Health, the buildings of downtown Boston, and as the sun rises, I'm finishing my hill repeats.

NEW YEAR

Thump, thump, thump, my footsteps. I see Faulkner Hospital, and think back to what Gary said about Dr. Trump's impending firing—"don't put things in writing."

And now I'm running down the hill, near the Arboretum bench. My father lives on—in John and me.

Home—John chortles, "Apa, it's the hundredth anniversary of selling Babe Ruth to the Yankees!"

January 7, Saturday 10:08 AM

Sunrise defies description with simple words—it looks almost nuclear in its colors, and makes me think of "Red Sky in the Morning, Sailors take Warning."

I recall the book review I read, a treatise about the Black Death, the plague of 1350, which reshaped society, and how we're in a similar moment, post-COVID, except COVID never ended.

I speak with Martin about UMass's 3-year MFA—it's free except you have to teach. He also told me he has a book of stories coming out—he's publishing with a small press. He'll have readings at bookstores around town. He pointed out that the big New York City publishers are all about money—can they make a killing off a book?

That's all they care about.

–

Margo and I go for a walk—chilly but beautiful. I carry a hardcover book by Jonas Sachs. "Story Wars"— those who tell the best stories will rule the future. And I think about the stories we could tell about Malcolm X—that we are working so hard; our patients are struggling, and we can't give them what they need in a brief 15 minute visit, and then all this MEGA mumbo jumbo. We take on the hero role—save the patient with HIV, save the patient with out-of-control diabetes, save the middle-aged man who is depressed, struggling with chronic pain.

And what happens is we burn out, because we're not working as a team, because the MBA types who run the health center don't know anything about patient care. They only know about squeezing us—pushing us to increase our "productivity."

I was born in Columbus, Ohio. My father had been in prison—the Shawshank Redemption movie prison, actually. But then he started taking computer programming classes and was released on furlough/parole to become a consultant. He worked full time and got his PhD at Ohio State. He worked as a business school professor, teaching MBA students management information systems for decades. So I'm not anti-MBA, but I am against exploitation.

My father died ~2 years ago, but if he were alive I know he would support me in standing up for patient-centered care and justice for health workers—treating us with dignity.

Margo and I walk by a neighbor's house, its enormous inflatable reindeer out front.

We have to stick together if we're going to make Malcolm X a better place.

Margo finds some yellow rice on the ground outside and starts eating it. "Hey," I exclaim, tugging at her leash.

January 8, Sunday 10:52 AM

John and I are sitting at the kitchen table and he is playing with his new "Strat-o-matic" baseball game, as I listen to some Coltrane. "Are you going to take Jon Lester out? It's the 8th inning," he says. I admire his shiny, straight brown hair, and take a sip of water from my Ohio State mug.

I think back to my conversation an hour ago with Balazs Varga at our sons' indoor soccer game. He runs a tennis academy for inner city youth. [It's hard to focus on my writing with John talking Strat-o-matic baseball].

Parenting and tennis—Balazs spoke about the price families can pay for being too obsessive regarding "excellence." Tennis elites are sometimes not on speaking terms with their parents—Steffi Graaf, etc. Bottom line—being a "Tiger Dad" might help your child become a superstar, but at a significant cost. How to support a kid without becoming a domineering parent?

-

I slept ok. Was up for a little bit at 3:30 AM. Ate leftover pizza and drank a lot of coffee. I was looking at Grand Rounds from a Stanford psychiatrist named Dr. Tricia Suppes, the former head of the International Society for Bipolar Disorders.

-

Walking home now, flurries. I didn't hear any great stories this morning. Then at the end of run, Ron was commenting on Suz's jacket, saying she is "like medusa"—he can't look directly at her, which led us down a rabbit hole of Greek myths.

January 10, Tuesday, 7:55 AM

I'm in the car, just having left the Reggie Lewis Center, and am driving home through Roxbury after a hard track workout. Barry Zelman and Sam Peters were there, and Barry asked about Dr Humble. So I told him the story of George's resignation.

I was having some arrogant thoughts at the end of the workout, that Sam is "just" a primary care doctor, and Barry is "just" primary care / preventive medicine—no advanced training like I have. I did an infectious diseases fellowship, and I also was in the Epidemic Intelligence Service at CDC. And yet the ABIM took away my board certification.

So I want Van to get his act together. But I also have to be Zen. Van said he's working on it, but it's been almost 5 years. A nudge wouldn't be terrible, but I'm so behind on MEGA; trying to write this book; trying to learn more about treatments for bipolar.

And I have to push my own lawyer—he reminds me of Preston J. Doublespeak, my father's lawyer decades ago.

As I drive, I also think about the story Barry Zelman told me—that his son made a fire in the fireplace but forgot to open the flue.

For me, prevention is about staying healthy, preventing mania and depression—not getting sick. That means managing my stress levels.

One other thing Barry told me is the last time he tried to do a track workout with Sam, he got injured from pushing himself too hard. And that rehabilitation lasted 8 months.

So don't go overboard, Dr Phil.

January 11, Wednesday 6:39 AM

Off on my run, trying to recover from my meeting with Dr. Roach yesterday. I tried to keep a positive attitude, but it's always bordering on a fight. And then I don't sleep well during the night, and probably the workplace toxicity has something to do with it....

And now, walking home after my run—the others waited up for me at a few points... I burned some energy.... And what did I learn? There's a Korean Netflix show about an autistic lawyer, Extraordinary Attorney Woo. A dog passes me, not on a leash, and then a man walks by.

"Very disciplined," I say.

"Yeah..." the man responds, with a laugh. "He's cold."

What else?

Pablo has to go to court today on Zoom, and it's hard to read the body language of the judge. I see a sign on a light pole for JP Improv—I did that class once. I have to keep improvising in my interactions with Dr. Roach.

Veronica was talking about a colleague she hates. "That's probably how my boss feels about me," I joke. So everyone has their challenges, if it's dealing with a derelict coworker, or MEGA.

But I run, and try to enter a Zen-like state.

January 12, Thursday, 7:35 AM
Running in the beautiful Arboretum this morning with Gary. As I run, the jazz standard "Doxy" is going through my head, and I try to synchronize my breathing with the music and the rhythm. It was a good run—I felt kind of stiff, and there was a dusting of snow so it was a little slippery, but the dark outlines of the hills and trees against the dawn sky are peaceful, along with the lack of cars.

And now, walking home, I'm thinking about last night's conversation with Jessie Texeira, the physician with bipolar, who detailed her struggles, including switching off lithium for lurasidone because of a creatinine bump. We also talked about our experiences with stigma and the feeling of being uncomfortable if you are in the closet—or out of the closet.

January 14, Saturday 5:04 PM
Jon Jefferies is dead, and I am cooking lasagna on a dreary afternoon as Miles Davis plays in the living room. Jon was my cousin's husband, and he had a heart attack while walking in the woods to see eagles.

I can't claim to know Jon well, because we never lived in the same city. But I liked him—he was always kind—jolly, even. I remember his big smile—at Aunt Pat's on Xmas eve. He worked as a photographer, I believe. He and Kellie and their boys lived in the Cincinnati suburbs. When my mom and I were visiting my father's grave last spring, we had hoped to meet up with Jon and their family, but it didn't work out. Now it's too late—and what will become of his boys?

The other thing was Jon was black—the only African American spouse of any of my cousins. My family was not overtly racist towards him, as far as I know, but I don't think we had an anti-racist orientation, either.

Anyway, I'll miss Jon's warmth, and this comes as the latest in a string of sudden deaths in my immediate family: my father, my grandmother, several others.

"Hey Apa—the guy who set the all-time RBI record was shorter than you and lighter than you—5'6" and 194 lbs," John interjects, patting my arm. We eat popcorn as we wait for the lasagna to finish baking. Thankfully, Margo isn't barking—for the moment. The radiator clangs, and Oma walks out of the kitchen, humming to herself.

"I want a snack," John calls out. I rub my forehead, pump some water for myself, then open my At-A-Glance—nothing on my calendar for tonight. I look at the next few days, then close it.

Shabbat is almost over—a working Shabbat, at Malcolm X with Angel Putzel, Julieta Veneers, and a nurse—a busy urgent care session with patients from Guatemala, Honduras, Puerto Rico, the DR, Cape Verde, the USA—a schizophrenic off her medications, a lady with a breast abscess, a woman wanting to be tested for Lyme even though she almost certainly didn't have it, a type 1 diabetic with arm pain, a homeless man on methadone with chronic kidney disease and hypertension—the list of my patients went on and on.

January 16, Monday 10:31 AM

I drop John off at Extra Innings, and I poke my head back in just one more time to see his wavy brown (chestnut) hair. He's a big kid.... There with all the other boys to play baseball on MLK Day. I'm thinking about my GPS, "Shirley," and John laughing as I drop him off, and my dad a few years ago with 2 GPS's going at the same time, so he could have a diversity of opinions. My father, Al, RIP.

I drive down Boylston Street, past the Guitar Center, where I might like to stop and purchase a big amp, past the Star Market parking lot, where Oma will pick John and I up after the ballgames at Fenway. Past the Ghost Bike and on to Riverway, Crazyway, Arborway, Jamaicaway, whatever you call it, it rhymes with Fenway.

The back of Beth Israel Deaconess Hospital, the House of God, where I used to visit Nimthaki, my friend, an ID doctor there. And I know every square inch of these trails from my running. And then I think about middle age, me 42, my wife older. Of course we can't slow down time, we can only hope to enjoy the present.

6:16 PM

Oma is mad at me, I guess—she says I am too negative about Dr. Roach and Dr. Trump, Malcolm X, about food, about everything, and she doesn't want to be around me so much. I think she is being hypercritical. I went to Pete's funeral earlier today, and his youth hit me hard. Younger than Kathy, just a bit older than me. I go in the other room and bring Margo to the couch, so I am not alone.

Oma comes in and apologizes—sort of. Sometimes I am too much, she says.

John comes out and wants to play soccer.

January 17, Tuesday 6 AM

I try to let go of last night.... to be even keeled... not the negative person that Kathy says I am, that I can be. This negative person she doesn't want to be around, the person who complains about Jo and Jesús. The person who is always hypercritical, saying that things are not right, that we should change things, for example by unionizing.

Is she accurate with her critiques of me, or is she more reflecting her own mood? I don't know, but I do believe that if I were trying to write my life story, I would want to be a rebounder, like the basketball player Dennis Rodman, perhaps. Someone who goes in a negative direction, but then bounces back. Relentless, persistent, even when things are grim.

And then, I consider the idea of ecopsychology, of being connected to the land, to Mother Earth, even as we mourn its destruction. To fight for the planet, for the sky, the trees, the soil, the rivers.

So even if Kathy is right, maybe I will follow my New Year's resolutions and treat her kindly, using the Golden Rule. And I'll also remember my other resolution, to be Zen, to keep breathing.

Now I find myself running in the Arnold Arboretum. There's a half-moon over Busey Hill, with stars and airplanes crossing above me in the dark. And as I continue up Peters Hill, the dark colors gradually change—into fiery oranges, yellows, reds, and light blue, and the light starts to reflect off of the snow. And all of a sudden, the cold darkness begins to turn into a new day.

Gary says goodbye, reminding me to share the robotics email

from our kids' elementary school principal with him. A real marathoner. I jog down Busey, followed at a distance by another older man, a speed-walker.

People are waking up, going out, moving about.

I think for a few moments about sharing the details of today's run on Linkedin, which I recently rejoined after a year's absence. A photo of my running watch, a description of our 5 miles this morning, the plan for the Providence Marathon in May. But then I reconsider—I've done that before. Social media posting, blogging.

And for what? This is a year for DDD. So I will be disciplined.

January 18, Wednesday 7:13 AM

I'm back from my run with Pablo, reflecting on our conversation. He does Yoga every night, following along with someone on Youtube named Adrienne. We also talked about workplace stress, and the tendency to demonize the other side in a conflict. It made me think of Dr. Humble and Dr. Trump.

And I'm thinking of mentoring and career development in the workplace—at Malcolm X are we just "worker drones?"

January 19, Thursday 6:46 AM

I'm back from my run through Franklin Park with Gary. Our conversation started with the coyote spotted outside the Arnold Arboretum School, and focused on fears: fears of wild animals, but I argued to him that cars are more dangerous to kids than coyotes—and the principal isn't warning the parents about cars speeding near us. Instagram is also dangerous, because of its impact on mental health.

But then our conversation progressed to Anti-Asian bias/racism in America, in our educational system and society at large. I agreed with him on this, and pointed out the historical antecedents—the Chinese Exclusion act of 1880s, Japanese internment during WWII, white supremacy.

7:13 PM

I'm a pill pusher, and I text Abdul for help—65 MME/day—it's a moral injury to keep refilling oxycodone for back pain... And he says >50 should go to pain management, or even >30 I shouldn't be dealing with. Primary care is ridiculous. American health care is crazy.

January 20, Friday 10:09 AM

I'm sitting in urgent care, waiting for patients to come... herpes on the mouth, foot pain, and COPD. I want to launch a protest next Friday to wake up my "sleeping" coworkers; I imagine myself outside in a white coat with a placard. A silent protest, with a statement and petition for community members and health care workers, calling for health care for all, patients over profits.

January 22, Sunday, 2:08 PM

I'm sitting on the couch with Margo, John, and Oma, digesting the lasagne and black bean soup that Dr. George Humble fed me. And Margo curls up next to me and John works on his college baseball bracket in his notebook, and Oma reads Catch-22 and laughs intermittently.

"Ok, Apa," John says, starting to fill in the teams on his bracket. Tennessee, Vanderbilt, etc, and I hold Margo's warm flank. I adjust my Ohio State hat, pulling it down below my ears, and run my fingers through my beard, trying to recenter myself.

What will Oma say, I ask myself, when I tell her what I've decided to do? James Meredith, Greta Thunberg, Dr. Quentin

Young, MLK, Gandhi, so many other heroes from the past, calling me to lead a walkout this Friday at Malcolm X Health Center for *Health and Healing*. Will Kathy be ok with it—a silent vigil/petition?

Can I get any others to join me, to follow me? And how will Naren, Bridget, Jesús, Jo etc react? Elmer too, our "enemies" (oops, I'm demonizing again).

And can I get the Boston Globe or our local NPR affiliate to cover our walkout? Or will it be a flop? Will it be enough to save Malcolm X from our imminent collapse?

Margo snores and John leans over his bracket. I advocated that the Buckeyes and Wildcats get high seeds, but I'm not sure he will listen to me.

January 23, Monday 7:21 AM

Margo looks at me, then licks her leg, again and again. She raises her eyebrows (do dogs have eyebrows) on her expressive face. Oma flushes the toilet, then walks into the living room, then back to the dining room and turns on the lights. She adjusts the photos of John and the family, which sit atop our piano.

Breathe.

I was up at midnight, eating cereal and honey, and skipped my morning run. No matter—I'll walk to work. I'll listen to jazz along the way.

January 24, Tuesday, 9:39 AM

Snow on the branches outside, and I'm happy to have closed MEGA and snapped shut my laptop. I get so grouchy when I am working with the electronic medical record—it feels like a moral injury to be delivering substandard care. And I'm outraged, but not many other people seem to be. Where are the protests?

So I do what I can do. I do a track workout with the running club, sprinting my hardest on the last 200 meter lap. I spend 2.5 hours on Zoom with the home health aides, who are committed to unionizing Malcolm X, when so few other people (doctors, nurses, etc) seem to be.

Together we go down our excel spreadsheet of 300 employees, line by line. I snuggle up next to Margo, touching my nose against hers (didn't the Care Bears do that in the 1980s?). The dog walks off into the kitchen, and I breathe. I once read a book about a young boy who survived Auschwitz—things might be bad at Malcolm X, but we aren't starving, and we aren't in a concentration camp. So keep things in perspective.

Margo hops back on the couch, does a little pirouette, opens her mouth and yawns. I hear Oma walking around in the kitchen, probably listening to the Catch-22 audiobook on her headphones. She shuffles into the living room, singing to herself—probably going to the gym now. "So happy," she says, doing a little dance. "Oh, chua" she says (Korean for cold). Hot pink gloves.

"Tomorrow I can't eat anything," she says. "I'm going to bring juice and gatorade—I have to work in the morning without eating anything. Am I going to survive?"

She has a colonoscopy in two days.

Margo puts her front two paws up on the couch armrest and swivels her head back and forth, looking out our window as Oma drives off. I feel my fingernails—they are too long. I need to cut them so I can play the violin.

I've re-centered myself, to a certain extent, after the morning's MEGA session. It's sad that the electronic medical record bothers me so much, but it really does.

I adjust my father's scarf, and Margo curls herself into a little ball and leans against the pillow. Catch-22 sits on a small table across the room from the couch. Yes, I feel like Yossarian, and no, I don't want to fly any more missions.

I sneeze, then scratch my face. My job feels Orwellian, and I have the sense that a Sword of Damocles is hanging over my head.

January 26, Thursday 6:55 AM
Back from a run—I got soaked, but now I'm warm and dry. And I'm not thinking about Ron's RV certificate, or my dream last night about meeting Marcus Williams in the airport. Rather, I'm pondering my friend Dr. Monica Potts's advice—that I take up gratitude journaling and positive affirmations (spoken out loud). She says there's so much moral injury at Malcolm X, we have to counteract it. Of course through advocacy/unionization, but also through mindfulness.

So I'm grateful I can run and play violin; I'm thankful for Oma, John, my mom, and Margo. And I make the affirmations out loud. "I am a good doctor. My patients are grateful for me. I help people every day. My coworkers respect me. My family loves me, and I love them. I'm helping contribute to the end of discrimination. I'm helping raise John, a good boy. All living beings are interconnected, and I'm putting my energy towards peace."

January 27, Friday 6:18 PM
Things are pretty miserable right now. Oma is giving me the silent treatment and I'm giving her the silent treatment. It feels like the worst conflict in our 10 years of marriage.

It started yesterday—Kathy's colonoscopy was delayed. Then she asked me to get chips for John when I bought burritos. And

I pushed back.

Then we had a couples therapy session by video with Dr. Park and I felt hurt. She seemed to be taking the position of Drs. Roach/ Trump—that I am 100% to blame for my problems. I just need to work harder at MEGA; don't be unionizing. I knew her statements were colored by her exhaustion after the colonoscopy, but they hurt. I know I'm a good doctor, father, and husband.

All day—nothing. No text messages from her to apologize, or even to try to compromise. And dinner was a silent affair.

I try to be Zen. But it hurt. Maybe because of her words. Or maybe because she's right? I'm a complainer.

January 30, Monday 11:26 AM

I'm at home, off work today, and John happens to be there too, out of school with an upper respiratory infection (COVID negative). Kathy and I made up on Saturday morning, and have been doing better since. I started texting her because I didn't want John to know we were having a fight, and that helped us resolve things. Then I went to a Malcolm X union meeting, which was successful.

Then yesterday Oma asked if we should go look at a little house for sale over near Green Street, and we spontaneously called our former realtor, and we made an offer, $785,000. So things certainly made a U-turn in 48 hours; we'll see if we get the house.

Now John is up from the dead, and healthy enough that he is going to watch his baseball on Youtube, despite this cough. My son giggles, sniffles, giggles. I look at his quasi-mullet, his bed hair, and smile.

January 31, Tuesday 11:34 AM

Sitting on the couch with Oma and Margo, getting myself prepared to go to work. This morning I had a neurology appointment at Man's Greatest Hospital with Dr. Brian Rosenberg—he had a surprisingly poor bedside manner, seeming rushed and grilling me from behind the computer screen. Eventually he lightened but still he talked too much, stressed by MEGA. At least he isn't forcing me to get a brain MRI. We'll see what Physician Help Inc and the medical board say.

I think about our busy lives. The new house is up in the air. John is back at school so that's good. Oma is "homa" from her workout at Mike's Fitness. I'm almost caught up on MEGA notes, although I have patients calling my cell for Ambien refills, open-MRI orders, etc. Oma pets Margo's ears.

February 1, Wednesday 7:13 AM

John is laying on the mattress on the floor, coughing, and making some shapes with his fingers. I'm thinking about the email I just sent to my employment lawyer, Hannah Folts, about the toxic atmosphere at Malcolm X, the micro-aggressions. I am proud I'm fighting back, even a little bit.

February 2, Thursday 6:48 AM

I'm back on the couch after a run where Ron was joking with me about the retirement of Dr. Phil, the TV personality. "He always made me mad," I tell him, "Because he was rich and famous and I am neither." What I didn't tell my running buddy is I am carrying around Dr. Phil's book in my backpack as motivation to publish my own manuscript.

"He'll probably run for President," I tell Ron.

"TV personalities."

It's the American way, in our hyper-capitalist society.

But another lesson from Dr. Phil's biography, as I understand it: he hitched his star to Oprah and she helped him rocket into the stratosphere.

I've hitched my star over the years to humbler people, role models like Drs. Jack Geiger and Hamza Brimah, people invested in community health.

February 3, Friday 7:02 AM

Sitting on the couch with John as he leads a baseball draft. "Ted Williams, I knew I was missing something," my son says. Margo stands in front of us and whines, wanting my son's egg sandwich, but then the dog licks his bare feet.

I think of my session with Anna yesterday—I read her some excerpts from my legal pads, my book's first draft. She said it reminded her of the movie "My Dinner with Andre." I vaguely recall watching it my senior year at Paul Laurence Dunbar High School during our zero hour seminar. But I don't remember what it was about exactly—a conversation over a long meal?

Margo runs after Oma and the egg sandwich, and John chortles. Now he's eating oatmeal with raisins and cinnamon. I hear the beep of the microwave in the other room and the hiss of the radiator and the sound of John shifting on the couch. I hear spoons clinking and pages turning in his "Baseball Hall of Fame Desk Reference."

February 4, Saturday 11:47 AM

Pro's and con's of the Roslindale house we just visited, vs staying where we are in Jamaica Plain—clearly there are trade offs. So the Roslindale place is huge, 3 floors, and beautiful, with a nice yard and proximity to the urban wetlands which reminds me of Michigan and my childhood. The downside—my commute would go from 3 to 5 miles each way, difficult for walking or running. I'd have to go by bike, which can be dangerous, particularly in the winter.

It would be fun to commute through the Arboretum, however.

Another downside—this house is bad for aging people. Lots of steps, no bedroom/shower on the first floor. And we'd still be at Boston Public Schools. The Arnold Arboretum School is sort of ok, but what about high school? And the money? We actually don't have that much savings, and my job at Malcolm X feels super tenuous.

Better to find a small ranch somewhere, a house like 2072 Oleander Drive, my Old Kentucky Home? And what about being locked down in Boston for 5 more years with a mortgage? I'm always Tijuana dreaming.... I'm tired of this toxicity from Drs Trump/ Roach, the difficulty of unionizing Malcolm X, the memories, the medical board. Staying put gives us the possibility of moving somewhere new... that being said, the wetlands house was gorgeous.

February 5, Sunday 8:17 PM

Thankfully we backed away from the "wetlands mansion"—I did love the backyard and the nearby park with its boardwalks, but my opinion is right now isn't the right time for that kind of change....

February 6, Monday 6:50 AM

Today I'm thinking about Carlos, my Spanish teacher and ping pong buddy at the ICA Spanish School in Quetzeltenango (Xela), Guatemala in 2003. Spanish was such a struggle during college, but then came easily at the ICA. And that launched my Latin

American travels, my interest in the U.S. / Mexico border, and forays into Portuguese / Mozambique.

I'm excited to go to Los Angeles, San Diego, and Tijuana in 2 weeks, and although I'm always "California Dreaming" and recalling the Bostich/Fussible Song, "Tijuana Makes me Happy." I'll try to remain satisfied with all we have.

What else? I talked with Matt Sabian last night and he told me about controversy between CDC and the Indian government over some tuberculosis maps he was making. And I told him about the book I am reading, "Age of Concrete," regarding Mozambique, and then an autobiography I am interested in, "Life: A Journey through Science and Politics" by Paul R Ehrlich, co-author of "The Population Bomb," published in 1968. Ehrlich believes that bringing down population numbers is necessary to realizing justice and creating a world with a chance of sustainability.

February 8, Saturday 7:45 AM

On the 16 Bus to Malcolm X (black ice) as walking is treacherous. Ron and I managed to jog a little this morning without falls. The question I have is how to get on the same page with may wife about our future—Massachusetts or moving to California. And the issue of trust—how can Kathy trust her husband, with his bipolar disorder, to be making logical decisions for the family, for John's future?

Our bus rolls by Glen Lane, White Stadium, the golf course where I usually walk. It takes about 15 minutes. What else? RIP David Harris, former husband of Joan Baez, who fought against the Vietnam War.

And Dr. Fanon suggested I go forward with the New York Times op-ed submission—*from the front lines of a federally qualified community health center (FQHC).*

Bus stop. "Stop Requested."

February 9, Thursday 6:50 AM
I sit, thinking about Tuesday's psychoanalysis session. If I'm going to pay $125 for 25 minutes of talking, I want to get my money's worth.... I don't need to let Drs Roach/ Trump's critiques affect me so much.... I'm figuring out ways to be more pugilistic, more creative, more entrepreneurial, tougher, even if my lawyers aren't excited about my case, even if the medical profession is stigmatizing. I'm doing some "positive fighting" with my YouTube videos. I'm listening to Kathy, I'm running, making music, life is good.... And the "Signifier," the word I will extract from today's session is "MUTUAL."

February 10, Friday 7:00 AM
I'm eating matzah in the kitchen after my run with Lester this morning. He never ran outside before—I hope he transforms himself.

Kathy looks at me, rolls her eyes, blinks, leans over. "What's funny? " she asks. "Me? Something else?"

She puts her coffee cup down.

"Communicate with me, not the paper... You're going to write that down too, oh my."

She heads off to shower, and I think about my neighbor who screamed out the window while Margo was barking, then followed up with a text message.

"This is the second time this week that your dog's barking has woken me up at five in the morning. No one is up that early. Please have more consideration for your neighbors."

I could point out it was 5:20 AM, but probably that isn't the best strategy.

Later
On hold. Patient needs a knee brace. Classical music. I need to fax something. "Thank you for returning my call.... I need a fax number." I sigh, hang up the phone. My MEGA Inbasket is flooded again with patient calls, results, messages. The life of a primary care doctor.

I wasn't always a PCP at Malcolm X. I had a previous stint in public health at CDC and also a few years as an ID doctor. But I got sick and was fired, so here I am, faxing a knee brace order. And then I need to order a patient a new cane, then call a patient with COVID-like symptoms, then put in a dermatology referral, then phone a patient whose MassHealth won't cover a bupropion prescription, then refill someone's omeprazole, a 90-day supply so insurance will pay for it. Yada, yada, yada, primary care in the age of MEGA.

February 12, Sunday, 7:48 PM
I'm eating grapes in the living room while listening to "Honeysuckle Rose," the recording by Claude "Fiddler" Williams. John is on the couch and Oma/Margo are in the Orange Room. Kathy's been in a bad mood off and on all day, but I hope she's pulling out of it. John had a temper tantrum early this morning and that threw her off.

I had a decent day—I ran 5 miles in the morning then 5 more in the afternoon, and I took a day off from MEGA. It's just too much to do it every day, even though I've fallen behind again and need to catch up.

The other new thing is I'm excited about making videos for internal medicine board review. I've been experimenting, making a few, and I like it because it's an opportunity for me to demonstrate my knowledge. But how to build an audience for "the other Dr. Phil?"

February 13, Monday 7:20 AM

I'm sitting in John's bedroom as he studies the sports section of the Globe. He's also reads a book at the same time.

I think about who else might help me with my goals, for example my neighbor, a retired labor lawyer with expertise in OSHA. Or Grayson, a Boston internist who assisted me with Physician Help Inc, 5 years ago—maybe he knows a lawyer who could spur Van and Hannah into action.

What else, I think, sipping my coffee? Oma says she didn't sleep well. I'm concerned about not having Dan Truman confirmed to take care of Margo while we are in California.

"Apa, I didn't notice you were here," John says, then heads off to the bathroom.

I spot my white coat hanging on the back of a chair in the dining room, and as I often do, my mind wanders back to my 2004 White Coat Ceremony at the University of Pennsylvania. Nanna and my dad were there.

February 14, Tuesday 7:13 AM

Valentines Day on the couch—Margo pokes her nose and whiskers up against me. John is in the bathroom and Oma is hastily getting ready for work. The dog hops up next to me and sniffs my ear, then sits down. My valentine :)

I bump my nose against hers.

"D-O-N-E" John calls out from the bathroom.

"Ok," Oma says, but not fast enough.

"D-O-N-E!"

He wants to be wiped.

Margo starts barking.

"Margie, Margie..." I say.

February 16, Thursday 7:00 PM

Teamwork is important, I think to myself, sitting in clinic. Today was a good day. I'm glad Van will petition the medical board. And talking with Lester was energizing.

Running together will help us.

February 17, Friday 6:55 AM

Los Angeles tomorrow! What do I want to get done before then? Clean up my MEGA Inbasket, of course. Hold the mail. Sign up for the LA 10K. Remind Dan Truman once more about the plan for Margo. Make the multiple myeloma video—my last before the trip.

Pack—clothes, passports (for Tijuana). Debit card, iPhone with charger, Audio recorder with batteries, violin, Lithium/Aripiprazole, toothbrush, watch charger, At-a-glance, music practice book, running book, money tracking book. I'll bring an extra legal pad, just in case I miraculously finish writing 30 pages during the week. Actually, maybe I'll text Dan to ask if he wants the crate, or if he thinks it's ok for Margo to sleep on his couch? But beyond packing for LA, what are my goals? To have a nice trip; to go to Tijuana (El Lugar Del Nopal).

February 18, Saturday 11:24 AM

We're on the airplane for a short flight to New York City, then a layover, then a longer one to LA. It's a full flight and we're still at the gate—John is smiling. I'm feeling cheerful too, getting ready to travel to sun-kissed Southern California. The pilot makes his boarding announcement, and I think back to the old days, pre-pandemic, pre-fatherhood, when I used to travel all the time, to Maputo, Lusaka, Windhoek, Addis Ababa, Havana, Mexico City, etc.

Lately we rarely travel—maybe the last time I flew was a year ago, to LA, and last April to Cincinnati and Toledo. Anyway, traveling by air brings me back to the concept of rootedness and home, and my question of why Kathy seems so attached to Boston when her family is in Los Angeles. It also makes me think of Otto Frank, since I just started reading the "Diary of Anne Frank." Exiled from Germany to Amsterdam, still trying to escape but unsuccessfully, then forced into hiding in the attic. Otto wanted a safe home for his family, but was foiled by the Nazis.

"Thank you, Apa," Oma says.

February 19, Sunday 4:18 AM (Pacific Coast Time)

I'm sipping instant coffee at Wayharmoni's 1-bedroom senior apartment in Los Angeles near MacArthur Park, as she offers me sourdough bread and John reads "It's a Numbers Game: Baseball." Oma is in bed, but my son and I have jet lag. He sneezes.

This place reminds me a bit of Anne Frank's hiding place in the attic in Amsterdam—small and cramped, with the 4 of us here. But it is lovely—Wayharmoni's photos, fake flowers, a "white Jesus" painting, a box for her diabetes and high blood pressure pills, framed pieces of art with Korean calligraphy on the walls, the smell and taste of her kimpop and kimchi, tofu, etc. Actually, I think I'll begin this dairy entry once more, and in homage to Anne Frank, who wrote to her "Dearest Kitty," I will begin anew...

Dear Albert,

Why am I writing to "Al"? Is this "Albert," Albert Lewis Lederer, my deceased father, who passed away in October 2020? Perhaps this diary entry will reach you through psychics, seance, or medium? Or maybe writing to the spirit of "Al" will give my entries more focus, a requiem? Anyway, "Al" is the new Kitty.

"Al," I thought of you yesterday while we were on a layover at JFK—the UK Wildcats were playing the Tennessee Volunteers at Rupp and I recalled our December trips in the upper deck, between 1995-2010. I don't remember any specific UK games, just the spectacle, and my favorite players, Anthony Epps, Wayne Turner, Walter McCarty, and the walks to the car after the games. The good old days :)

Well "Albert," here we are. You're resting in peace, and I'm eating a banana at my mother-in-law's. Time flies when you're having fun.

So, "Al," what are my goals for this trip to California? To have a nice time. To go to Mexico, ideally spending two nights in Tijuana so I can get the pulse on what's going on down there. But today my plan is to drink coffee, to enjoy Wayharmoni's breakfast of apple and avocado slices.

"Ou-you?" Wayharmoni asks John. "Do you want milk?"

All for now, "Albert." Best wishes.

Yours, Phil

February 20, Monday 6:03 AM

Dear Al,

Again I'm drinking coffee at Wayharmoni's after a fitful night of sleep. But we had a great day. I ran my 10K race in the hills of Elysian Park above Dodger Stadium; then we went to Porter Ranch. John enjoyed making a "family tree" with one uncle, and playing catch with the other. And watching my son's cousin with his autism, I felt grateful for John's health. I nibble on one of Wayharmoni's barley snacks, hoping to get my bowels moving. I want to run a few miles before we take our bus to San Diego.

Yours, Phil

February 21, Tuesday 10:26 AM

Dear "Albert,"

We're on the border, on the Playas de Tijuana boardwalk, looking out at dolphins frolicking in the Pacific. "The waves are so big," John exclaims, and it's true. High tide, and they are crashing on the tiny beach. The border fence stretches out into the sea, and ~16 miles north of us we see the skyscrapers of San Diego. "The tide is going down," John remarks, and I look around. Maybe it's the wind, but there aren't many people out on the boardwalk (even though it's sunny). A few seagulls float above us, and just like the dolphins, they can cross the US-Mexico border freely, but people cannot.

You could imagine a high speed "lancha" setting out from Rosarito at night, evading ICE and landing at Pacific Beach or Torrey Pines, but who knows how often that happens. The border is tighter than when I moved to San Diego 15 years ago, that's for sure.

"Tu mereces cumplir todos tus sueños," someone painted on a building above the Playas boardwalk. "You deserve to realize all your dreams." John and I retreat to a bench.

Yours, Phil

February 22, Wednesday 7:41 AM

Dearest "Albert,"

We are atop Hotel Jatay in the restaurant, and it's a windy

morning. "I hope Pujols gets a hit and Longoria is up," John says. More baseball. But then we learn the restaurant doesn't actually open until 8:30, so we are evicted back to the 3rd Floor. At least they give us coffee.

I listened to Democracy Now earlier this morning—Dr. Ira Helfand, a colleague from Western Massachusetts and advocate for the abolition of nuclear weapons, spoke.

So no run along the ocean this morning because of the high winds and waves in Mexico.

What else? We had a nice time yesterday with my Tijuanense friend, eating at his restaurant, then driving along La Revo, and through the colonias and hills back to Playas de Tijuana. In his SUV, things seemed safe and normal. He didn't talk about gangs or drug lords, and his only reference to violence was an oblique comment that some colonias are dangerous. But then I told him about the shooting on our street in Jamaica Plain and he was horrified. Danger is wherever guns and violent people are.

Yours, Phil

February 23, Thursday 10:59 AM

Dear "Albert,"

We're at the Science Museum near the USC campus in LA, and it's crowded with kids. Noisy, too. And seeing all these children makes me think of the quality of science education in our public schools. Of course this should be America's highest priority, but leaders like President Biden seem more interested in grandstanding, beating their chests, and inching us even closer to Armageddon. What if there was a "peace studies" course in our public schools, where kids learned the history of pacifists, organizing techniques, etc? Perhaps then, humanity would have a chance.

There's so much potential power in these kids.
But will anyone speak up for justice? Will I?
Yours, Phil

February 21, Tuesday 10:26 AM

Dearest "Albert,"

I'm sitting on the couch at Wayharmoni's digesting the papusas I just ate—bean and cheese, with coleslaw and hot sauce. It's been heavy downpours all day, with flash flood warnings, although I got a 3.2 mile jog in. I also finished Anne Frank's "Diary of a Young Girl"—of course she was discovered. Her words and her personality do live on, and I'm left appreciating the tremendous stress the people hiding in the annex were under. They coped as best they could, and Anne stayed sane through her journaling.

"Oma, down here," John whines from the thin mattress on the floor, but she demurs, saying she is too full right now, papusas.

I hear cars honking from near MacArthur Park, down below us, and I burp. Being hemmed in by this nasty weather makes me feel like Otto Frank.

The other thing that was sad about Anne was the amount of conflict between her and her mother. I hope we can keep things peaceful in our family.

Oma reads "Slaughterhouse Five," and John rolls around on the bed.

Yours, Phil

February 25, Saturday 6:28 AM

Dearest "Albert,"

Heavy rain continues, and it's chilly, so as much as I want to get out and run this morning, I haven't gone yet, instead eating a leftover papusas as John sleeps. If I do run, it will be with the hope that I can find a CVS to buy an LA Times. It's Shabbat so I'm keeping my phone turned off today, but I wouldn't mind reading the news.

Rain, rain, go away. We only had 2 sunny California days on our vacation, and we fly back tomorrow. I did run 3 miles yesterday in the rain, so it's ok if I don't run again until Monday.

I haven't done much music on this trip, although I brought my violin. At least I am writing, and I read Anne Frank's diary.

John is sleeping—so much hair.

I'll be like Otto Frank—stoic, and here for my family, whatever happens. Probably we'll stay in Boston, which is ok.

Oh, Dr. Humble texted me yesterday implying Dr. Trump is being fired. And Dr. Roach emailed saying Jesús is only "on leave." So strange.

Yours, Phil

PS- 1:30 PM

We're at the food court of the Science Museum and Oma gave John tangerines and koguma (Korean for sweet potato). A pizza is coming, to my chagrin. I am glad he likes the museum, however.

I know it's Shabbat and I should be relaxing, but I can't get my mind off work. I'm thinking of downloading the doodle app and setting up a poll with other health workers in Boston. The idea is a white coat protest for single payer, racial equity in health care, public schools, and anti-war, a fusion event.

But it's Shabbat so I'll try to relax and enjoy this Saturday in Los Angeles. I eat one of John's tangerines and drink some water.

February 26, Sunday 4:44 PM

Dearest Albert,

We're at about 15,000 feet and ascending out of Charlotte after a mad dash to make our connection. John is eating a pastry, Oma is reading Slaughterhouse Five, and I'm listening to Sonny Rollins.

Also I'm thinking about Ernie's text message—I'd suggested to him that we ought to revive the Medical Committee for Human Rights, which was around in the 1960s. His answer was what is the value added when we already have organizations like Physicians for a National Health Program, Physicians for Social Responsibility, etc? My answer is MCHR would add some energy and history to our work. We would be able to advocate for an anti-war platform without the constraints of PNHP/PSR. We could protest for reproductive rights, Black Lives Matter.

Yours, Phil

February 27, Monday 6:54 AM

Dearest Albert,

We're back in Jamaica Plain and I finally slept well after a week in Los Angeles and during the windstorm of Tijuana.

John emerges from his bedroom, shuffling along.

"Good Morning," I call out, but no response.

Margo trots around.

"Glad to be home?" Oma asks, and John smiles, hugs her, then grabs the Boston Globe. It's spring training.

I'm alone on the couch, listening to the radiators. I think about what Gary told me—on Sunday, March 26, there is a "Bus Run" along the Boston Marathon course. My Providence Marathon preparation definitely needs a long run.

What else?

I want to cook something good, with tofu or broccoli or quinoa.

Gary says it will snow tomorrow, but that's ok. The mornings are getting lighter, and we had a nice sunrise.

Yours, Phil

February 28, Tuesday 2:42 PM

Dearest Albert,

I'm sitting in the provider workroom at Malcolm X getting frustrated. Being a PCP at a community health center = constantly getting shat on. Patients are falling through the cracks, nurses are burning out, pharmacies are dropped from the insurance network, patients have homicidal ideation and are taken to the ED by the Boston Police Department.

We have no leadership.

But it isn't as bad as Mozambique. My friend Natinho Nunes sent me a WhatsApp message that there has been severe flooding around Maputo. Where is the World Health Organization? Where is the United Nations? People are drowning, getting cholera, etc.

Meanwhile, my MEGA is overflowing once more.

As I wrote in a letter to the editor to the Globe a week ago, "physicians and other health care workers should organize and unionize, before it is too late."

But we don't have a meeting scheduled. We are dawdling.

Yours, Phil

March 3, Friday 6:36 AM

Dearest Albert,

Today I wanted to write about birthdays. Because today is my grandfather, Paul Neuser's birthday—he would be 103 if he were alive. And Sunday is your birthday, dad; you would be 77.

So Paul, "Pete," was born in Ohio in 1920. He flew on a bomber during WWII in the Pacific, then worked on the highway for his career. He was a gardener, painter/artist, and dog lover. I remember the poodles, Taffy/Teddy and Ginger, and the stories about others. And of course the tale that he would give coffee to his dogs.

How time flies. I remember Christmas, Thanksgiving, and Easter at Rockingham and Rollins Road when I was a child. I remember my grandfather's voice, his laugh. But I'm no longer a kid.

And your birthday, in two days? I'll try to remember you as well.

Yours, Phil

March 4, Saturday 8:48 AM

Dearest Albert,

A hunger strike for health care justice. That's what needs to happen. Felipe Portillo did it regarding environmental justice, and it worked out ok for him. He didn't get sick, and didn't lose his job, even.

And I was reading the New York Times this morning, a story about two Thai activists on hunger strike who are close to death, Tantawan "Tawan" Tuatulanon, age 21, and Orawan "Bam" Phuphong, age 23. They are fighting a law that criminalizes critics of the monarchy, and for reforms to the Thai judicial system.

It feels right. The only problem—2018. As part of my mania, I started "fasting for Ramadan" in solidarity with the Palestinians. That was not a good situation, and Oma will freak out if I announce a hunger strike to protest the American health system.

First step—meet with Felipe Portillo.

What else? Dr. Jesús Trump was officially fired yesterday. It seemed like Naren was saving his own ass, because Bridget Wilson was promising to fire him if he didn't fire Dr. Trump.

Also, Jorge Martinez emailed me, that Park Eun-Bin has cancer.

There's a lot more to say there, particularly how Oma reacted to the email. But let's leave it for now. And back to the hunger strike. It's most likely to succeed if I practice fasting for one day at a time, drinking only water. And if I study the physiology of hunger strikes, particularly around lithium and kidney function. And if I can get Monica Potts, my best friend at Malcolm X, to do the hunger strike with me—two doctors doing it is more likely to have an impact than one.

But I also have to clear my mind and focus and be like Oscar Robertson, whose memoir I am currently reading.

Yours, Phil

March 6, Monday 5:52 AM

Dearest Albert,

I'm not running this morning because I went 13+ miles yesterday, then played indoor soccer with John, Wilfredo Varga, and his dad Balazs. I spent most of the rest of yesterday in bed reading about Oscar Robertson. And John was excited to teach me the Korean card game Hwatoo. I found it challenging—all the different ways to match cards reminded me of the neuropsychological testing with Dr. Runtsky.

Yesterday would have been your birthday, Al. I showed John a cute video of him on your lap, age 3 at Harbor Point, playing the train game, "Going to Milwaukee." Choo-choo, he bounced along. He remembers you.

Sara Norton from MassCare emailed me back—we hopefully

can talk about single payer on Wednesday.

I'm 15 notes behind in MEGA—I didn't do too much this weekend. But I will catch up. And I think we have a union meeting today.

Harry Campo remembered your birthday yesterday—I'm grateful to him.

I emailed Jorge Martinez about Park Eun-Bin—so that fire seems to be out, for now.

Yours, Phil

March 7, Tuesday 3:29 PM

Dearest Albert,

I'm at Malcolm X, awaiting my meeting with Dr. Roach, after bumping into Angel Putzel. She hates technology, particularly social media for kids. I recommended the "Mindful Tech" book by David Levy, but the question is how to implement his advice, looking at ourselves as we use computers and IPhones.

For me it's anxiety-producing to know I'm 10 notes behind, but at least I know I'm not alone, and I'm writing about it. Dr. Fanon suggested I write rather than go on a hunger strike and decompensate.

What else? Andy Krister, our financial adviser had my mom, Kathy and I on a zoom regarding $4000 in shares, and I saw my mom stumbling and tried to get everyone to end the zoom. She doesn't do well with videoconferencing. We need to protect her dignity—a poet who sputters with words.

Yours, Phil

March 9, Thursday 6:44 AM

Dearest Albert,

I'm back on the couch after a 5-mile run with Ron, Gary, and

Veronica (how could I forget her name), along with Veronica's dog. We talked about Anne Frank's hideaway in Amsterdam, and Veronica's recommendation regarding a novel for me to read, "The Idiot."

Ron talked about his recent safari, and that made me think about the sympathetic nervous system—*fight or flight*. Human beings need to run much more—it's in our DNA—sometimes wild animals do chase us.

Last night Ben Benson came over for some old-time banjo/-fiddle tunes which was good, and then I chatted with Monica Potts about Malcolm X.

Most important in life is figuring out a way to stay Zen. Dr. Fanon would say to write. Dr. Beck would say to talk to Kathy. Bob Parker would say to play my violin, sing, and listen to music. Millie would say to lift weights and box. Dr. Park, to take Kathy's perspective. Anna, to use art to express myself.

Yours, Phil

March 10, Friday 6:37 AM

Dearest Albert,

Back from a 5 mile run with Ron and Gary—chilly, but a nice sunrise and I was happy to be out on my feet. I brought up the robotics club, thinking of MSTC, and Gary basically said he's too busy. But I don't want to give up, so I'll email the principal asking if interested parents would respond to a Doodle poll for a meeting.

I'm doing this for you, dad, who slept in a car in Pittsburgh for 2 days to try to get me into the top public magnet school in the city. I imagine the robotics club like Odyssey of the Mind, OM, which I participated in in Michigan as a kid. Enrichment is key.

And I'll email Belinda Contreras, the music teacher at Arnold Arboretum School. And see if Dr. Roach can change the time of our meeting so I can attend the Spanish Club.

Yesterday I had a nice day. I enjoyed planting radishes in our front yard raised bed, then sitting in the garden with the sun on my face. And boxing with Millie. I'll keep fighting.

Also, Sandhya, Sara and I are talking about writing a perspective to submit to the New England Journal of Medicine about reviving the Medical Committee for Human Rights.

Yours, Phil

March 12, Sunday 11:00 AM

Dearest Albert,

I'm in the kitchen, drinking coffee, listening to John's baseball, thinking about the reports Drs. Jesús Trump and Jo Roach submitted to the medical board.

Painful, but that's ok. No surprise they wrote critical things. Life is a battle. I need a strategy, to organize people to support me as I try to have the restrictions removed from my license. Would Dr. George Humble help me? Dr. Monica Potts?

The bottom line is America's healthcare system is messed up.

Yours, Phil

March 13, Monday 7:03 AM

Dearest Albert,

Red sky in the morning, sailors take warning. I just returned from a 5 mile jog, after yesterday's 16 mile run with Sam. And the sky is a mix of orange, red, pink—I guess a storm is coming.

I'm thinking about Angel Putzel being my new Physician Help Inc monitor, when there are plenty of others who could play that role at Malcolm X. Should I push back against Jo Roach? Or just cross my fingers and see what happens?

I picked up John a couple of books from the Little Free Library—one about soccer, one baseball—I'm so lucky to be a dad. I'll figure out a way to engage with the Arnold Arboretum School—I think they are having a meeting of the health and wellness committee.

Yesterday John was so cute—wanting to make a "Post Office" Board game, and drawing a world map when we were at Grandma's. The mail carriers will deliver the mail. No matter the obstacles.

Speaking of my mom, I am convinced she has primary progressive aphasia from dementia.

Yours, Phil

March 14, Tuesday 6:49 AM

Dearest Albert,

I'm sitting with John in his bedroom during a torrential downpour, listening to Miles, "On Green Dolphin Street." The sax soloist blows up and down through his licks and arpeggios. John reads his soccer novel; it is a peaceful moment. And I'm happy because Oma is back in a good mood. Yesterday she was grouchy because John didn't want to go to school and the dog was barking.

Now Miles is playing the head on his wobbly, muted trumpet—glorious. And the song is over.

So today—I'll go to the gym, have psychoanalysis, cover Wendy Anderson's MEGA Inbasket because she is on vacation, clean up my own Inbasket, meet with Dr. Roach, email Van. La Lucha Continua.

Yours, Phil

March 16, Thursday 6:51 AM

Dearest Albert,

Oma and John are hugging and laughing which is good to see, because when I woke up this morning the toilet tank wouldn't fill with water. I'm not a Home Depot kind of guy, so I'll probably be paying $200+ for a plumber to fix a fill valve.

Oma is leaving at 7:10 AM because there is a conference; it is precepting week. I just feel this distance between us—not sure why.

Margo comes up and noses at me, which makes me happy. Then Kathy walks by, vigorously brushing her teeth, and we both laugh a bit.

She wanders off, and I look at her butt, her breasts through her skirt, tights, fleece, and imagine her naked, us making love.

"You keep staring at me," she says, giggling, and wanders into John's room.

"The weather is supposed to be nice," I hear her say.

Love is weird.

Margo sits next to me, loyally, as the radiators hiss. I think of my conversation with Babe Cohen last night. Life is a boxing match — or a marathon.

John and Oma admire the tomatoes he planted, and she turns on the grow light.

Yours, Phil

March 17, Friday, 6:00 AM

Dearest Albert,

I'm just trying to release my negative energy toward Kathy, after she rejected me last night. It isn't entirely her fault—it is her biology.

But why doesn't she prioritize a relationship? There's minimal desire, spontaneity, creativity, so it seems. Once we do get going and make love, it is good, but she seems to forget about that the other days. Instead, she falls back into the same, hackneyed trope—"I'm too tired."

But why doesn't she wake up early? Why doesn't she realize the nefarious effect of burnout, and the American health system, on her psyche and get therapy, make some changes?

Why doesn't she realize our lack of frequent lovemaking—or love—has an impact on me? The way she acts, it seems like she doesn't care about resuscitating our relationship? I find this irritating—but maybe I am just selfish.

Yours, Phil

March 18, Saturday 8:24 AM

Dearest Albert,

I'm at Forest Hills, waiting for the 16 bus to take me to Malcolm X, ruminating on my ongoing beef with Kathy. Last night she was watching YouTube videos until 1 AM. I am a good person, with a job, funny, and am in good physical shape. So why is she rejecting me? Options include: 1) Her depression, 2) Her age/menopause, 3) Exhaustion, 4) Stigma against me because of bipolar, or 5) she doesn't love me like she did before. 6) A combination. 7) Or, something from my end.

Stigma she can be educated about. Depression related to her job as a primary care doctor dealing with MEGA is hard. We already have a couples therapist who encourages us to take the other person's perspective. We could get a sex therapist, if Oma would agree, which she wouldn't. It's frustrating! I'm 42 years old and healthy, and I want to love, and that seems to be a low priority on her end. Garden, card games, YouTube videos, cleaning the house, MEGA—those get energy. But our marriage?

ROR, to quote "The House of God." ROR = Relationship on Rocks.
Yours, Phil

March 19, Sunday 7:07 AM
Dearest Albert,
My life is a roller coaster—things are better with Kathy. We had our Argentinian friends over for dinner last night, Fidel et al, and then later, Kathy and I made love, now my amorous outrage has dissipated.

So I'm going to run 17 miles today—4 over to Juan Gonzalez's house, and then we'll drive down to New Bedford for the half-marathon. My goal is to feel strong, not get injured, etc.

Kathy comes into John's bedroom, and announces, "I like my house," then comes over and kisses John a few times. I sip my coffee, and look at the morning sunshine.

I remember you, my father, your resilience from prison back to grad school at Ohio State.

I have similar resilience—psych ward back to becoming a marathoner. A writer.

Life is all about having a growth mindset. Perhaps being diagnosed with bipolar is the best thing to have ever happened to me.

Yours, Phil

March 20, Tuesday 10:26 AM
Dearest Albert,
I'm leaving urgent care soon—I might talk to Dr. Crow about our frustrations, then Kathy and John are picking me up at 12:30 PM.

The morning was ok. First I had a telemedicine call with a patient with COVID—I gave Paxlovid.

Then I saw a woman with schizophrenia/bipolar, whose friend tried to bite off her thumb.

Then, a man who had a recent ED visit, and needed some reassurance.

Then, a Cape Verdean woman with ear pain, chest pain, and no period recently.

Finally, an older Dominican woman with fibromyalgia.

I'm convinced that our health system needs reform, and the only way that will happen is if we get white coats in the streets.

Yours, Phil

March 23, Thursday 7:18 PM

Dearest Albert,

It's been an unexpectedly tough week, but I'm doing better, Oma seems to be uninfected, and John is cured. Let me explain.

COVID hit John first, Sunday morning, but he only had the sniffles. Then Tuesday at lunchtime I got sick—chills, headache, sore throat, cough, and a temp of 100.8. And I felt exhausted.

I spent the next 2 days mostly laying flat, and only this afternoon did I go for a walk with Margo. Two, actually. I'm still exhausted and congested but hope to jog 1 mile tomorrow morning.

Meanwhile, controversy in Boston Public Schools—rates of those who head to college have gone down. Gary seems ready to decamp for Newton.

Kathy and I had a good couple's session with Dr. Park. Zen, inner peace, needs to be my focus.

Yours, Phil

March 24, Friday 3:19 PM

Dearest Albert,

Day by day. I'm improving gradually. I did run 1 mile today! Some sneezing and runny nose but I think I've turned the corner. Maybe I can still run the Salem 20 on Sunday, or maybe the 10 miler.

Margo and I went for a nice walk. I made 2 videos, one on legionella and one for World TB Day, based on Matt Sabian's work. And I was interviewed by a medical student about prisons and antimicrobial stewardship. As always, it made me think of my dad. Professor Resilient.

I've been enjoying this Buddhist monk, "Venerable Nick," on YouTube. I think he is right—chanting, meditation, alms in the morning.

Margo barks a few times in the living room, and Dexter Gordon plays his sax. Meditate on death in the morning. Ancestors in the evening. These rituals are important. And Ramadan just started, Monica Potts told me.

Yours, Phil

March 25, Saturday 6:16 AM

Dearest Albert,

I'm sitting here looking at a black binder, an assignment from 8th grade, 1995. "My Life: An Autobiography." 28 years ago, wow.

The cover is decorated with green, yellow, and gold paint. The book itself is 32 pages long, typed and double spaced. Chapters include "My Favorite Holiday," "Fun St. Patrick's Day Parties," "A Gift I'll Never Forget," and others.

The last chapter is, "If I had 3 wishes." I talk about slavery, poverty, famine, drugs, sweatshops, and my desire for "everyone to be happy." And for stress levels to be reduced. And "good health for everyone."

This might have been the first time I wrote about the right to health, March 22, 1995, in 8th grade at Morton Middle School in Lexington, Kentucky.

28 years later, I feel the same.

Yours, Phil

March 26, Sunday 1:58 PM

Dearest Albert,

Margo trots over to the radiator, stands up on her hind legs, puts her front paws on the metal, and looks intently out the window toward the street. She barks, then returns to the wooden chair in the corner of the living room.

I glance at my iHealth rapid antigen COVID test. It's day 5, and I still see the faint line—gonna still be positive for COVID.

Margo jumps off the chair and returns to the radiator, barking wildly.

"What are you worried about?" I ask her aloud. She only barks in response, then sits next to me on the couch, sniffs me, and yawns.

"I should be your dentist," I tell her, and she licks my chest. "Stop that," I say, and scratch her neck.

John and Oma are still playing cards in his bedroom, and I listen to their banter, then rub Margo's whiskers.

Life is good. I'm glad I was healthy enough to run 10 miles this morning. Maybe I'll be back at Malcolm X tomorrow, after this little unexpected sabbatical.

Margo curls up into a ball.

Yours, Phil

March 27, Monday 8:42 AM

Dearest Albert,

NEW YEAR

I open MEGA and groan—so much work to be done. One patient needs ketotifen fumigate ophthalmic solution refilled. Another needs Spiriva actuation mist. Another needs bisacodyl. Another requires oxycodone. Another has 2 prescription requests. There are 19 patient calls, 10 results, 120 staff messages, 11 open charts, 16 cc'd charts, 3 patient advice requests, 10 scanned documents, 25 outside events, and 13 outside messages. Plus 35 overdue results and 3 prior authorizations. And 9 prescription responses.

Yours, Phil

March 29, Wednesday 6:52 AM
Dearest Albert,
"You won't ignore me," I say, rubbing Margo's head. Kathy is on MEGA, her back to me, and John is in his bedroom with his breakfast and the newspaper. I'm irritated with Oma for serving him food in his room—it's antisocial; why can't we eat breakfast together as a family? I'll try to sit here with that sense of annoyance.

Why am I experiencing that emotion? Maybe because I get so little time with my son, and I'm scared he might not come home from school someday, with these school shootings and feckless President and members of Congress. I feel powerless.

My best idea is to start a parents/caregivers book club at the Arnold Arboretum School, to organize the parents.

It's a marathon, so I will try to keep lobbying the most likeminded—Sally Varga, etc, with my little flyer—"Come join the book club."

Yours, Phil

March 30, Thursday 7:12 AM

Dearest Albert,

Kathy is not in a good mood—she feels "blamed" when I talk about John eating breakfast in bed, dinner in his bedroom, refusing to walk home from school, refusing to write in his YouTube baseball notebook, quitting violin, piano, cello—a lack of discipline. She says these kind of things are "on me"—I need to negotiate with him, tell him to get in a routine of eating in the kitchen.

She slides a book in front of me, without a word—"How to Talk so Kids will Listen and Listen so Kids will Talk"—by Adele Faber and Elaine Mazlish.

I push it away.

But I pick up the book again, flip it over—harmony in the home—only if Kathy, John, and I all "buy in." And things are chaotic at school, I'm sure, so how to establish a calm home?

Kathy says our routine is improving—he is showering, wiping himself, etc.

Yours, Phil

March 31, Friday 7:02 AM

Dearest Albert,

A plate just fell in the kitchen, and Margo jumped off the couch to investigate. But it didn't break, and now John is eating his breakfast, a waffle, while studying the morning Globe. The baseball statistics, of course.

The sun hits my eyes—it looks to be a nice morning, even though it's cold. Margo stares at John's breakfast, and my son coughs a couple of times. I'm just trying to be mindful of the moment; meditation through writing, pen on legal pad.

But then I sneeze twice.

Margo scratches herself.

I try to be still, as my guru, the venerable Nick, advises.

I see my shadow on the living room wall. That's life—reality, and what goes on in the shadows.

Our son sings to himself, coughs again, and draws a little bit on the sports page.

"John, it's 7:11, what time would you like to go to school?" Oma asks.

Yours, Phil

3

April Fools

April 1, Saturday 7:16 PM
  Dearest Albert,
  Well here I am, with my new laptop, a Macbook Pro, listening to "On Green Dolphin Street," again. Margo is collapsed next to me, and I stroke her paws, the nails, the muscles of the foreleg.
  And I inhale slowly, adjust my hands behind my head. Shabbat was an odd one today, but here we are, Saturday night.
  I rub Margo's whiskers and she twitches.
  "Oma," John calls from his bedroom, but I don't hear him clearly. I turn down the volume. "Oma or Apa?" I ask.
  "Oma," he says. "Ok," I respond. And I hear some noises from the kitchen... that's where Kathy must be. The volume goes back up.
  The piano is tremendous... I have no idea what the chord progressions are, but I hear them coming along with the melody, and the steadiness of the upright bass.
  "Oma," he calls again, and I listen to the trumpet. I feel my fingernails extended out over my fingertips, and I type some more, then I touch Margo's nails.

The song ends. Water running in the kitchen. Some sort of bird chirping outside. A siren in the distance. My feet on the pillow. Margo's legs.

Water, again.

This is what it is like to be present, to breathe, to feel your fingernails on the keyboard of a new computer. To pet your dog.

"Oma," he says, again.

"Way," she replies, in Korean.

"Come."

Yours, Phil

April 3, Monday 7:34 AM

Dearest Albert,

John's bedroom is clean—books on the shelves, notebooks lined up, clothes folded in the basket, balls in their box, and he's reading a Matt Christopher book. His oatmeal sits on the bedside table, and he takes a bite now and then. Oatmeal and raisins.

It's a sunny morning, and I slept in, because I ran 15 miles yesterday, which was tough because of residual COVID congestion. Then we worked in the community garden, then saw my mom. She had called and said she was "sad" because we hadn't been there for a while (COVID). Her emotions are more up and down, and the question is if we can help her with her finances, or day-to-day activities (a sitter)?

These are the concerns of modern life. A mother with probable early Alzheimers. The quality of the Boston Public Schools. Keeping love in a marriage. A difficult job as a physician; a history of trauma and mental illness.

Yours, Phil

April 5, Wednesday 6:53 AM

Dearest Albert,

I'm sitting in John's bedroom, and he is talking about the Red Sox while lounging on the floor. "Pittsburgh has Mitch Keller on the mound," he tells me. I look at his hair, his chocolate-brown eyes.

"Maybe we should stay with Paxton into the the 3rd," he says, "but we don't want to waste a mound visit."

I drink some water, clear my throat, lean back in my chair. Take four deep breaths.

Time amazes me—it keeps racing forward, no matter how much we want to freeze it.

I start to worry about my clinic, and my medical license, but I come back to the moment. Four more deep breaths.

John is sitting on the blue bouncy ball I found on the side of Washington Street.

Four more deep breaths.

"Hedges, on the inside pitch, jam fly right," John announces.

Mindful time. John leans against my leg for a moment. Passover today. Easter coming up.

"Fly, way back. Verdugo can't make the catch!"

Yours, Phil

April 6, Thursday 8:03 AM

Dearest Albert,

Oma is acting oddly—she has a telemedicine visit with the family practice Physician Assistant at 8 AM for a variety of symptoms—headache, vomiting, weakness, "Brain fog." I think it is stress, perhaps with a touch of gastroenteritis. She has been discussing if she needs a head CT, or bloodwork? To me she needs to exercise, eat well, have social interactions, and find a way to fight back against the medical-industrial complex which is threatening our well-being.

It's Passover, and I think we need a redemption song.

Yours, Phil

April 7, Friday 10:00 AM

Dearest Albert,

I'm back in the workroom in primary care, after what felt like a useless set of morning meetings. Our health center leadership is focused on money, for example "capitation reimbursements," rather than health equity.

So here's a letter, based on MLK's Letter from a Birmingham Jail, except my letter is from the Malcolm X Health Center "Jail," and I'm imprisoned by my job here, as well as Physician Help Inc, and the medical board.

But it's a long walk to freedom, and just as my father (you) were imprisoned in Mansfield, Ohio—Shawshank, and developed patience, I will too.

Yours, Phil

April 10, Monday 6:37 AM

Dearest Albert,

I'm back on the couch with Margo on a sunny Monday. Kathy stops by and asks if she can have the primary care residents over on a Thursday evening in May. Ah, Tufts—it reminds me of that day in 2018 when Sonya came into the ED, and Hashim Ghazali and I saw her, the concern for hemorrhagic fever. That situation triggered my downward spiral from which I have been trying so hard to recover.

Over the weekend, I found her grave in a cemetery outside town, and I want to visit it, to pay my condolences. She was so young.

It was a preview of what would happen two years later, for real, with COVID—a pandemic.

John goes back into his bedroom, where he is ensconced with the sports page. The Red Sox swept the Tigers.

Yours, Phil

April 11, Tuesday, 6:59 AM

Dearest Albert,

The mornings are getting sunnier which is nice, and I'm trying to focus on my goals. In particular, my New Years Resolutions, and my primary aim, to be more Zennish. I've been trying to do the 4 healing breaths throughout the day, to lower my stress levels.

I scratch Margo's belly and she looks at me out of the corner of her eye. I hear John singing in his bedroom. The microwave beeps—his oatmeal.

I have Dr. Fanon today, and I'm going to type up this journal entry. I want to go forward with this book...

Kathy stops by and tells me stories of her dreadful on-call last night—she was paged 7 times, 1:30 AM, 3 AM, etc, and it disrupted my sleep as well. Why would anyone want to be a primary care doctor?

Yours, Phil

April 12, Wednesday 7:39 AM

Dearest Albert,

I'm sitting at the Forest Hills lower busway, just having learned the next #16 bus comes in 21 minutes. Argh. At least it's sunny.

I'm distracted by a teenager to my right, but I'll try to focus on my diary entry. The biggest stressor—getting to clinic on time and seeing 11 patients in 3.5 hours without being overly anxious. An impossible task in the age of MEGA, but I will focus on the 4 deep breaths when I need to use them.

The only patient I can remember on today's schedule—Carl, an African-American man who reminds me of my father. I can't rush him.

"Have fun!" That's the advice I give John every morning before I go to work and he heads to school. Even when tasks seem filled with drudgery, we need to focus and "Have fun!" For me, in clinic, that might mean taking a moment and sketching a patient's face. Or sharing a joke with a family member. Or learning a new word in Spanish.

Yours, Phil

April 14, Friday 4:49 PM
Dearest Albert,

I'm on the playground at the Arnold Arboretum School, watching John, Wilfredo, and Mack kick a ball around; they just got it down from the tree where it was stuck.

It's sunny and the leaves are coming out; I rub my eyes—pollen, maybe. Dust rises from the woodchips on the playground. The Friday afternoon is winding down—and next week we have vacation.

Les puts a purple cup on his head and makes a face. He sits on the play structure holding a stick.

The kids score a goal and dive in the dirt and scream. Oh, to be young again. Birds overhead. A crow? I'm not sure. Mack fakes right and goes left. John steals it but Mack gets it back and dribbles.

Yours, Phil

April 16, Sunday 8:14 PM

Dearest Albert,

I'm exhausted, even though I'm on a vacation and didn't do much today. Maybe it's my mom—I'm coming to realize she may well have dementia. Her word-finding issues and anxiety seem so indicative. So I do what I can.

I'm on the couch with Margo, listening to "Have you seen Miss Jones," the jazz standard recorded by Chet Baker, and am thinking about the harmony. Breathe.

Today was a good day. I watched John's soccer game—he had fun. I played fiddle tunes with Ben Benson—another New Years Resolution, one step closer to our CD. And I talked on the phone with Mia, another doctor with bipolar. Perhaps I helped her a little. Yes, we need to write a wellness plan, and today is focused on exercise. I did a little weightlifting.

Yours, Phil

April 18, Tuesday, 6 AM

Dearest Albert,

Eliud Kipchoge lost. Yesterday, John and I watched the Boston Marathon to see the best runner of all time, our hero—but he fell behind on Heartbreak Hill and was defeated by Evans Chebet. Kipchoge is human, and by losing in the waterlogged race, we see him not as the superhuman who ran a 1:59 marathon, but as fallible. Everyone can stumble (he finished in 2:09) but he retains his dignity. And, like the Phoenix, he might rise again.

Kipchoge reminds me of my low points—the manias, my firing, my father's death. But as Kipchoge fell behind, he kept running.

At mile 23, John and I leaned forward as the trucks and motorcycles went by, and then Chebet and several others passed us, and no Kipchoge in sight. But then we saw Eliud, and he never gave up.

Yours, Phil

April 20, Thursday 8:32 PM

Dearest Albert,

I'm listening to Billy Joel, "Piano Man," the famous harmonica introduction. I just got off the phone with my mom—she reminded me you liked his music.

I'm dealing with intrusive thoughts—Jo Roach sent an email I found irritating, about my vacation coverage. So I'm trying to change my mindset—how can I redirect my anger into something productive—my violin, my book, unionizing, or marathon training, or all of the above. It was just this email atop all the crap going on at Malcolm X...

Yours, Phil

April 22, Saturday, 7:55 PM

Dearest Albert,

It was a good Shabbat. I ran 9 miles in the morning, then we had the Little League parade, complete with singing of "Take me out to the Ballgame," then John's first game. And I finished a book, Johann Hari's "Stolen Focus," which was good, and although I question some of the science he cited, I think his thesis was solid. We are losing our ability to focus, to maintain our attention, and some of it is Silicon Valley's fault, but not all. My takeaway—get a plastic "Ksafe," to lock up my IPhone for a period of time. Everything else seems bigger picture and societal—although I do want a 4 day workweek. Stress reduction. Reclaiming our democracy. Oh yes, and I unscrewed the lightbulbs in our bedroom—turning it into a cave could be good for our sleep hygiene.

Today is Mary Anne's Yarzheit—remembering "Bruzzie" (you) giving her eulogy in 2019. And us staying in the RV.

Yours, Phil

April 24, Monday, 6:50 AM

Dearest Albert,

I'm sweaty—this morning's run was led by Gary and Pablo which meant it was fast—but I kept up until the end, and now I'm listening to the birds. Margo is sitting at the front door.

Deep breath—meditative, slow writing. No need to tell stories or jokes or to hook the reader—the idea is just to sit.

Emotions come, worries arrive, but they go. I do my morning chanting, hearing my voice in my chest.

So the goal this week is to follow my wellness plan—exercise, food, sleep, being 'Zennish,' growth mindset, music/art/writing, etc.

Oma brings in the newspaper. "Oh great," I exclaim, because I know John will be happy to read the sports.

Yours, Phil

April 25, Tuesday, 6:54 AM

Dearest Albert,

The Devaney truck is rumbling outside our house, reminding me of my inability to stop our burning of oil and to replace it with heat pumps. A moral injury.

If it were cheaper to install the heat pumps… maybe I should get a new quote from New England Ductless? What's holding me back? It feels like I'd be doing it alone—also, I'm not 100% convinced of the science, that the manufacturing of these pumps, and generation of the electricity in old-fashioned power plants would be much better than our oil boiler?

I could ask a scientist I know, my friend Thomas Lloyd... he's also a musician.

During this morning's run, Suz talked about the chaos at her child's elementary school—Boston Public Schools—students and teachers in the halls, "screaming." I wonder if that's the case at the Arnold Arboretum School?

How to get parents together to join my book club, so we can have some discussions about BPS—quality, equity, class sizes, etc?

Yours, Phil

April 26, Wednesday 4:07 AM

Dearest Albert,

I'm up early which I'm not happy about, but it was a fitful night of sleep. Yesterday's meeting with Dr. Roach and Angel was tense. Jo was criticizing me for a number of things and I was feeling attacked; Angel was the "peacemaker."

Thankfully I had a good evening, going for a walk with Danny and playing baseball with John. Still, I worry about the impact this stress is having upon my health (and Kathy's).

I'll keep unionizing Malcolm X, but my only other options seem to be 1) to file a grievance with Human Resources; or 2) to ask to cut down on my hours.

Why am I not quitting, given these micro-aggressions? I've developed fulfilling relationships with a number of patients—one of them, a man with Crohn's disease, was reaching out to me late in the afternoon.

Yours, Phil

April 28, Friday 4:37 PM

Dearest Albert,

I'm at the Arnold Arboretum School, decompressing from last week. The Physician Help Inc saga continues—thanks to Dr. Roach, I have to get evaluated by a monitoring company regarding my clinical skills.

The kids are yelling, swinging on the monkey bars, bouncing basketballs. The sun has vanished into the haze, and I'm left contemplating my last patient of the day, a lady who came in with supposed bedbugs, and this made me think about delusional parasitosis. She also has a significant trauma history... A sparrow flutters by, reminding me of my mom's recent birdwatching. What used to seem dorky now is cool.

Enrique and David are chatting; Jeremy, who works for the MBTA, ambles by—the Arb parent community. "See ya, Phil," he says.

I look up toward the sun—Andrew Huberman from Stanford wants us to get more bright light (natural light)—it's good for the brain and body.

Yours, Phil

April 29, Saturday 5:47 PM

Dearest Albert,

I have neck spasms—torticollis—after working in the clinic this morning. I also decided to file a complaint against Dr. Jo Roach. Who knows how this will end up.

We're going over to Gary's house for dinner—John is already there. Apparently he played well at the baseball game.

I spot the Germany Lonely Planet I picked up from the Little Free Library—it makes me think of you, dad. What would you say about my saga?

You were very practical—saving money, advancing in your career. But you also supported me on my adventures—Guatemala, Mozambique, etc.

Kathy walks by, looking at her indoor plants. "These didn't really sprout," she says to herself.

Margo stares out the front door. I hear her nails tapping on our floor.

Yours, Phil

April 30, Sunday, 4:49 PM

Dearest Albert,

I just got off the phone with my cousin, whose husband Jon Jeffries dropped dead 3 months ago. She is grieving, coping, trying to keep going through the darkness for the sake of her kids. It reminded me of losing [you], dad, and the memories—you singing 'Puff the Magic Dragon,' to John when he was a baby. Time, loss, grief...

I'm waiting for Ben Benson to come over with his banjo... we'll have an old-time session, enjoy some tunes... Fiddle tunes cure the blues, even on a rainy day. Problems at work, my mom, conflict at home, a barky dog...

I'm Dr. Phil the fiddler, and I have my old-time tunes.

Yours, Phil

May 3, Wednesday, 7:01 AM

Dearest Albert,

Back from a run, watching Margo walk by, getting ready for clinic. John is excited—the Red Sox won—Connor Wong hit two homers. I need some mental toughness, to be like Wong, as I deal with the stress at Malcolm X. But I have some tools to keep me Zen, like breathing, chanting, singing, violin, sports, writing, friends and family.

Bob wants me to practice "Have You Met Miss Jones" in all 12 keys, around the circle of 4ths—I need to find a little time to do that when I'm not too tired (the evenings). Last night I didn't practice violin at all.

Dr. Fanon pointed me in the direction of decolonization in terms of dealing with the Physician Help Inc/Malcolm X crisis, and that was helpful. There's a power imbalance there, and I have little autonomy in the medical board issue; but I refuse to be exploited.

Yours, Phil

May 4, Thursday 3:32 PM

Dearest Albert,

Van and Hannah talked, but the legal stalemate continues. So I emailed Gilberto Soares, a civil rights attorney, and he promptly replied. But he said he couldn't take my case without evidence of discrimination. At least I'm still fighting.

Kathy did something nice just now, she took me to the garden and showed me our plot. We have sunflowers planted alongside corn, kale, etc. It was beautiful to see how we are connected to the land.

I look at my six New Years Resolutions, and amazingly I'm making progress on all of them. And Sunday, with some mental toughness I'll complete the Providence Marathon.

Margo walks over to me and climbs up on the couch. I love this dog. Her little whiskers, especially. You rub them and she turns her head.

Oh, and I got goggles! I'm going to go swimming.

Yours, Phil

May 5, Friday 8:00 PM

Dearest Albert,

I'm on the front porch with Margo, at dusk, and Oma and John are in the garden. I call Grandma but it goes to voicemail—I hear *your* voice on her answering machine and I leave a message.

I think of a GoFundMe to raise money for my legal fees for Van and Hannah, and the Physician Help Inc skills assessment. I could tell my saga...

Grandma finally answers and is listening to opera. Grandpa liked Madame Butterfly, she says.

"It's making me sad, except your dad liked it so much I got him the CD."

John and Oma come in as it gets dark, and he speaks of pollinating flowers.

Yours, Phil

May 8, Monday 7:39 AM

Dearest Albert,

I'm at the Forest Hills bus station after a terrific weekend. The Providence Marathon was a success—I was joined by my college friends Farley (Minneapolis) and Marvin (New York City) for the race weekend. We hung out on the Brown campus, eating East Side Pockets. Twenty years has flown by.

And, the race. It was sunny, so it was tough, but I kept going, down the East Bay Bike Path, past the carousel, the Rhode Island Country Club, then back along the bay into Providence. Tough but successful!

I was helped by Miguel, a 69-year-old retired speech pathologist and former 3:30 marathoner turned race walker. He blasted jazz ("I'm Beginning to see the Light") on his speakers and paced me for more than 10 miles through the heat.

And now that I've completed marathons in MA and RI, I'm

inspired to go for all 50 states. Maybe I can complete them by the time I turn 50 or 60.

Yours, Phil

May 10, Wednesday 6:15 AM

Dearest Albert,

I'm back from a jog with Margo and want to write about the "Marathon Mindset," a term I used yesterday during my psychoanalysis session with Dr. Fanon.

That is, in life, there are a lot of obstacles (aka crap) that come up. In running, the weather is hot or windy/rainy/freezing. Your earphones break or you get cramps. But with the "marathon mindset," you improvise, you slow down for a while, you take a different approach. The same with problems in the workplace or issues at home. The "marathon mindset" is like the "Growth mindset," except with a focus on long term gradual change.

I've decided to go for 50 marathons to try to build political commitment for a single payer.

Yours, Phil

May 11, Thursday 6:42 AM

Dearest Albert,

I'm sitting with John, back from my first run since the Providence Marathon. He's reading the Boston Globe, a story about the pitcher Kenley Jansen who just reached 400 career saves.

He sings to himself, eats his yogurt, coughs. "Apa, can you put this over there?" he asks, handing me the container.

Then, of course, Margo shuffles over and sniffs at it. These are our mornings, the quotidian events that matter so much. A sunrise. A boy who adores baseball. A dog with funny whiskers.

Forget about the $15,000 clinical skills assessment Physician Help Inc/the medical board are making me do. Stay here.

John tells me something else about Kenley Jansen.

Yours, Phil

May 12, Friday, 5:27 AM

Dearest Albert,

The birds!

I decided to start a daily morning meditation again—it's been a while since I quit attending the COVID Zoom meditation group. So I woke up, sat on the front porch, set my iPhone alarm, and closed my eyes. What was apparent was the songbirds!

They provided a cacophonous melody as I breathed in and out. It was glorious. I wasn't thinking about their chirping, I was just sitting with nature.

Today I'm going to send the email to HR with my complaints.

And I'm going to keep working on getting this skills assessment set up, even though it makes me angry. I am present with my anger.

Many of us Malcolm X health workers—Dr. Crow, Dr. Potts, Dr. Guevara—are upset. A threshold has been crossed.

Yours, Phil

May 14, Sunday, 11:07 AM

Dearest Albert,

Mother's Day—Grandma smiles when we give her zinnias and marigolds from our garden, also flour for her to bake bread with. She prepares tea for us—Bengal Spice, and I look around her apartment—the books, the wooden kitchen table from my childhood, her plants. I think of Nanna, her mother, my grandmother, passed on, buried in Toledo. I watch Grandma shuffle back and forth.

Yours, Phil

7:29 PM

At Fenway in the bleachers with John, the Red Sox tied 1-1 with the Cardinals. The sun is setting and there's a bit of a cool breeze. I remember Tiger Stadium in my youth, meeting Nanna at the ballpark. Those days of Cecil Fielder and Lou Whitaker.

Back in Boston, John leans against me, studies his scorebook. Nanna sometimes spoke of her favorite player, Charlie Gehringer.

Dejong from the Cardinals homers; John and I lean against each other, shivering.

May 15, Monday, 6:43 AM

Dearest Albert,

Back from a run, having discussed with Martin/Veronica a pressing question—if last night's journal entry, where I used the word "lean" twice, was excessive. Their conclusion was it might or might not work, depending on if it was building toward a theme (parent-child huddling together for warmth). So it wasn't necessarily careless.

Martin also pointed me to a famous essay by John Updike about Fenway, perhaps one of the most well-known things he has written. Well, after our late night at the ballpark, John is still sleeping, and I'm hanging out with Margo.

And I'm thinking, now, about Upton Sinclair's book, "The Jungle," because health facilities have become the modern sweatshops and are in need of an exposé, like the meatpacking industry in Chicago 100 years ago.

For instance, the patient I saw a few days ago who had just lost her son under unclear circumstances and needed help with bereavement, with finances, and even with meals, yet MEGA was prompting me to click the checkboxes to bill her insurance.

Yours, Phil

May 16, Tuesday, 6:54 AM

Dearest Albert,

Yesterday was good—I had the day off, went for a walk with Danny, hung out with Margo, had a violin lesson with Bob. We're moving forward with the book club, and John and I hung out on Danny's rooftop for his 40th Birthday Party. John liked the cider, but not the pomegranate juice.

And this morning, another run, through the Arboretum, past the lilacs. And now I'm back home, thinking about today—meetings with Dr. Fanon, Dr. Roy Basch, Angel Putzel. Marathon mindset.

My other idea—to email Donald McNeil Jr, formerly from the New York Times, for advice—journalistically speaking—on my saga. A doctor gets sick and gets punished by the system—Physician Help Inc, the medical board, employers, the American Board of Internal Medicine, insurance companies, etc. But Kathy, a private person, might be hesitant. I'll write an email to McNeil, but go over it with Dr. Fanon first.

Yours, Phil

May 17, Wednesday 6:39 PM

Dearest Albert,

After my run this morning, I picked up a book from the Little Free Library, a novel called "The Proposal" by Jasmine Guillory. Its back cover described it as a "charming, warm, sexy gem of a novel," and "witty." It starts off with the protagonist being proposed to on the Dodger Stadium Jumbotron—and her saying no, then starting an affair with someone else. Escapist, but fun.

How I wish I could escape from my nightmares with the medical board, etc—a summer beach novel like "The Proposal." And maybe I will read it, putting down my book about estate planning. We already have a will.

Dr. Fanon suggested I hold off on the email to Donald McNeil Jr, and instead think about what I enjoy about being a doctor—putting on the white coat, sitting with a patient, hearing their story.

Yours, Phil

May 18, Thursday, 6:54 AM
Dearest Albert,

"Voices of hope in a critical time" is today's theme, assembling a color 1-pager to help us unionize Malcolm X. Because things are getting more tense, we need to be more effective at recruiting people. We need a Mass Meeting, not painful zoom meetings. The question is when?

At my house, if Kathy is ok with it, on a Friday night after soccer. I need to edit the 1-pager I already have and add more photos—of Maria, Nancy, the others.

We need power! Power from people coming together.

We are making progress, but the December 31 deadline I've imposed for myself is looming. We have to be realistic. Unionization isn't going well. We are weak, and could be smashed by the Malcolm X administration.

Yours, Phil

May 19, Friday, 6:47 AM
Dearest Albert,

Iced coffee, post run, on the couch. I could write a bunch

of things about my conversation with Veronica and Gary this morning—ChatGPT, humanism, teleology of knowledge, gender—but perhaps instead I'll relax.

Put pen to legal pad, pause... refocus... and try to write down my memories. For example, of John and you, circa 2018, at Harbor Point, #307. Together you are reading books (which ones—maybe "Pickles the Fire Cat")—and you slap the book cover shut upon completion, which gets a laugh from the 4-year-old. He loved his Grandfather.

Life is so fleeting! You turn around and you are in your 40s, bald, with a mental health diagnosis, pills, therapists. Still marathoning and fighting for survival, but aging.

Margo licks my hand, then grunts. The sun through our window—winter turned to spring...

Yours, Phil

May 22, Monday, 6:44 AM

Dearest Albert,

Margo started barking, so I shut the front door and pulled down the blinds—and the living room is dark orange, shadowy.

Be pragmatic. After a weekend of struggling with what to do about Physician Help Inc and the medical board, I think of what you would say.

You'd tell me to pay the money, do the assessment. It's ok to keep writing, but I have no choice but to go along with Doctor Evaluation, Inc.

Margo sits next to me, tries to lick my ear, sniffs my legal pad. My ace in my back pocket is to go to the New York Times, but today my plan is to inch closer to signing the agreement with Doctor Evaluation, Inc.

Yours, Phil

May 23, Tuesday, 6:54 PM

Dearest Albert,

Pain.

Kathy said something along the lines of, "I feel like you don't think about your family so much."

I'm not exactly sure why—probably just stress from Physician Help Inc and the medical board, but she blames me. I'm accused of not working so hard on MEGA like she does.

Maybe she's thinking that I am so preoccupied with social justice that I don't see how it is hurting her and John. She wants me to be a MEGA Robot Doctor? Then at home to do the dishes and laundry and pay the bills and happily accept whatever sex comes my way?

Maybe she's right. Maybe I am egotistical and don't pay enough attention to my family.

Or maybe I am a human being.

Yours, Phil

May 24, Wednesday, 7:49 AM

Dearest Albert,

I'm at Forest Hills awaiting the bus; it's chilly but sunny. "Have fun, I love you," I told my family a few minutes ago.

"Have Fun," in American medicine? So important, but so hard in the brokenness of our health system, as we try to avoid the toxicity in the workplace.

"Have fun," when your expertise is denigrated by your superiors.

But I'll keep trying to connect with patients.

Yours, Phil

May 25, Thursday, 1:34 PM

Dearest Albert,

I'm on the Orange Line, on my way to see Hannah in her office downtown, on the 15th floor of a law office building on Federal Street. I feel like I've been transported into a John Grisham novel. And I don't like it.

Where am I headed in my journey? Will I lose my job or keep it? Will I lose my medical license or keep it? Will we succeed in unionizing Malcolm X or will we fail?

The train is crowded, and few of us are wearing surgical masks. For the most part you wouldn't even know a pandemic had ever happened.

I'll keep fighting for health justice, like the Soviet dissidents who were forced by the KGB and psychiatrists into a vicious cycle of false mental health diagnoses to discredit them. Many were reported to have "sluggish schizophrenia," treated with antipsychotics, admitted to mental hospitals.

Yours, Phil

May 26, Friday, 7:45 AM
Dearest Albert,

I'm at Forest Hills in the sunshine, thinking about letters and greeting cards. Nanna was always the most prolific, and my mom wrote many as well. From you, only a couple of notes survive. For example, a letter you wrote me in 2010. I resolve to write more letters to family.

Yours, Phil

May 29, Monday, 6:29 AM
Dearest Albert,

Memorial Day, breezy. I'm off work, thankfully. But I have a cold (COVID negative x 2), and haven't run since Friday. The cough was making me anxious on the drive to Nantasket Beach (Hull, MA), so I collapsed on the sand and finished Michelle Obama's new memoir.

The First Lady's lessons—have "a kitchen table" of friends; "When they [critics] go low, go high." People who are different are often discriminated against, but keep fighting. Take up a hobby to keep you calm (hers was knitting). When child rearing gets tough, keep going.

Except for my illness, the weekend has been decent. Friday night I drove down to Providence for my 20th Brown reunion. It was nice to see a few friends, and play some fiddle tunes on the Pembroke Campus with Harry and Farley, especially "Maysville" (JP Fraley). We traded a few stories, tossed a frisbee. Two decades since graduation. Glad to have my own "kitchen table" of friends, and I'll keep nurturing them.

John returns to his bedroom with a bowl of cereal. In May 2003, when I graduated from college, I wouldn't have imagined I'd be a dad.

Yours, Phil

May 30, Tuesday, 6:30 AM

Dearest Albert,

Slight course correction—I just ran for the first time in 4 days, 2.7 miles, and it was tough! I was coughing as I jogged along—it felt like I had pneumonia (I don't). I need to take it easy, rest, and recover.

Aww, shit!

I just poured my iced coffee on my bare chest. Margo glances at me, curious.

Back to my first New Years Resolution—Being Zennish. I think about the zen of running. The zen of old-time fiddle. The zen of parenting. And yes, even the zen of doctoring. What do they have in common? They can be relaxing, or stress inducing. Both will occur, but the goal is balance. When the stress-inducing events occur, the idea is to "adjust our sails." As they say, you can't change the winds.

Margo chews on her harness, so I unsnap it and pull it off. I hear Kathy whipping up eggs for John.

Yours, Phil

May 31, Wednesday, 9 AM
Dearest Albert,

I'm a doctor, doing the unsustainable, coping the best I can. But will I be able to stay well under this stress?

I'm in the clinic, exhausted, thirsty, and coughing. I do my best to breathe, to slow down, to listen to the patient during our 15 minute visit. But I'm concerned.

Will I miss something buried in MEGA? Will he get sick as a result? Many of my patients only speak Spanish, Cape Verdean Creole, or other languages, which is enjoyable for me, but makes the visits run long. And it's a busy morning—I'm going to be late throughout the session. I worry. I scowl.

I try to focus on the patient. He has hypertension, hyper-lipidemia, primary hyperparathyroidism, and other problems. I like him. He's a sweet old man. He worries about swelling around his ankles, and I reassure him—he needs to get some compression stockings. And obtain a home blood pressure cuff so we can come up with a better plan for what to do about his antihypertensive medications.

But as the visit goes on, I start to feel drained. Patients are beginning to back up, and I'm delivering half-assed care, even as I try my best to slow down. He leaves. Next. I log into MEGA.

I think about my advocacy for health justice over the years. I keep fighting, but it seems to be in vain. Is it about my ego, or the patients and the disparities? I don't know.

The U.S. spends more than $4 trillion a year on health care, yet life expectancy lags behind many other countries. The way America handles health care is unsustainable, for families, for clinicians. The racial disparities haunt me.

Being a doctor during COVID drove me to become suicidal, and a psychiatric ward admission. Painful memories.

But things have changed. I'm older and *presumably* wiser now.

Yours, Phil

June 1, Thursday, 5:37 PM

Dearest Albert,

I'm in urgent care. My first patient, who was reported to have hand pain, didn't show up. And now I'm waiting for the next one, a woman with schizophrenia on and off medications. And a recent intentional overdose, who was admitted under Section 12.

Erin pokes her head in the workroom—"light schedule," she says. We laugh.

Therese sits across the room from me, entering an order for Eloquis (apixaban) for a mutual patient with a blood clot. That lady had been receiving Lovenox (Enoxaparin) before, but had a procedure and the medication was changed.

I wonder about Therese. She's the sweetest, nicest person around. And she's been at Malcolm X for 30+ years.

Will I stay here that long, when every day things feel grimmer and grimmer? Is there a social connection, a community to sustain me here? I don't think Therese and the others here have been treated with dignity.

Yours, Phil

June 2, Friday AM, 7:05 AM
Dearest Albert,
I'm walking Margo, thinking how I'll get this book across the finish line. DDD. Cars race by on South Street, going somewhere. But how will I get where I want to go? I don't know any literary agents. I can write, but would anyone want to read my musings?
The dog and I pass Juicy Greens, Fiore's, and Curtis Hall, the heart of Jamaica Plain.
Margo sniffs, and I do too, lilacs?
I think about my patient last night, the man with knee pain, and a probable meniscal tear. I'm glad to be walking along with good knees. Grateful, not to have to get an MRI, see an orthopedist. Maybe the "finish line" is an illusion.
Yours, Phil
5:03 PM
It looks like it might rain, and the temperature has dropped from 90 to 70 degrees in an hour. Plus the mosquitos are out.
Dylan is juggling the soccer ball a bit but retreats to his IPhone. Mike dribbles a basketball, standing next to David. Wilbert climbs on the play structure while the older boys start up a pickup soccer game.
I text one of my patients, a lady with particularly bad depression and social isolation.
Bridget talks to another mom, as I hear distant thunder.
The soccer game heats up, and the rain is still holding off.
One of the boys heads the ball out of bounds. Stoppage of play.
My patient texts me back. She's coping.
Blackbirds zoom across the playground.

June 4, Sunday, 11:03 AM

Dearest Albert,

Kathy is planning to eat Sanukiya Somen, Japanese Noodles, and I raise my eyebrows—it has 1750 mg of sodium. Oh well; don't judge her dietary choices. Or, if I'm going to judge, I should keep it to myself.

And now she is telling me about her plans for our trip to Seoul in August—it's going to be an adventure, with Korean baseball, a Buddhist temple stay, etc.

I'm thinking about my New Years Resolutions—being Zen-nish, but I want to publish this book, and record a CD with Ben. We'll include the Clyde Davenport song, "Puncheon Camps." I can envision recording the fiddle tunes with Ben, burning a CD. But how will I block out the time to type up these legal pads? That's one of my main challenges, time management, when I'm so behind on MEGA and have this medical board sword of Damocles hanging over my head. I'm in the doldrums.

Yours, Phil

June 5, 4:46 AM, Monday

Dearest Albert,

Another legal pad, and I remember how you used to sit around with your own legal pads at 2072 Oleander Drive, Lexington, Kentucky. Often you were on the computer, and sometimes on the phone as well with one of your students—Bob, Skip, Henry. 1994-1999, my adolescence.

I recall my high school years, my stint working in the tobacco molecular genetics laboratory at UK, the cross country meets, orchestra concerts, Wildcat basketball games. The trip to Berea with Nanna and the other "Toledo-ones."

You blink, and that era is gone, the people are gone. Flash

forward a quarter century, and there's a little brown and white dog, an 8-year-old baseball loving kid, a garden-obsessed wife. A 72-year-old mother who stumbles over her words but still bakes bread, swims, and goes to concerts.

I lean into Margo. Yesterday, I finished reading a book called "Another Appalachia, Coming up Queer and Indian in a Mountain Place," by a Boston Public School teacher named Neema Avashia. The book resonated with me, and not just for its mention of Frank X Walker and the Affrilachian poets my mom used to speak of.

It's the idea of identity—Neema grew up in West Virginia, not quite fitting in, and I felt similarly in Kentucky, with its evangelical Christianity. But wherever you go, there you are, and my love of fiddle tunes was rooted in the years we lived there. Even yesterday, when I played a duet with Ben, I was brought back to an earlier, more innocent time.

Yours, Phil

June 6, Tuesday, 7:14 AM

Dearest Albert,

I'm feeling something after my run up Larz with the crew. Last night I was emailing with Harold, a nephrologist who has bipolar disorder, takes lithium, and is training for a marathon. Harold said he would hold the lithium the night before and night after the marathon. But even so, myoglobin released during the race will likely lead to some degree of acute kidney injury. This was disturbing for me, as I am frightened of developing a kidney problem. So I'll set up a nephrology appointment at Man's Greatest Hospital. Argh.

What else is bothering me? This car insurance paperwork from last month's fender bender. At least no one was hurt, and damage was minimal.

At Malcolm X yesterday, many patients canceled, so I only saw three—an older woman who's trying to control her diabetes with okra; a younger patient who is at high risk for HIV; and another patient with depression reportedly due to the "Imposter Syndrome."

Yours, Phil

June 7, Wednesday, 6:57 AM

Dearest Albert,

Today I'm thinking about shame and stigma. When I google myself (which I do frequently), one of the first links I see is the medical board website with its strong language –

The Board therefore alleges that the respondent has practiced medicine in violation of law, regulations, or good and accepted medical practice...

The Statement of Allegations has no context, however. It doesn't say that I was hired under a 100% full-time clinical contract; and that my new boss, Dr. Bush, told me that my job was going to be "undoable" the first time I met her.

It doesn't stay that from February-June 2018, I was working so hard to help my patients, inpatient and outpatient infectious diseases; tuberculosis clinic; general internal medicine clinic, community health center; that I didn't realize I was getting sick.

My mania was occupationally-induced, and the medical board decided to shame me, a "scarlet letter."

Yours, Phil

June 8, Thursday, 6:33 PM

Dearest Albert,

One of the hard things in primary care is the oxycodone scripts;

when a patient "grandfathers" to you on an extremely high dose (270 MMEs) and you are obliged to continue it. The medical director says so, but your friend, a pain management expert, states you need to taper it. It's a Catch-22, an impossible situation.

What else is hard is when your mother develops word-finding difficulties.

Yours, Phil

June 9, Friday, 6:52 AM

Dearest Albert,

Off for my run around JP... I start alone; Lester isn't there... I pass Pondside Dental (they sponsor John's Little League team) and I jog toward the pond.. I think about the email I received—anti-LGBT graffiti was just discovered on the outside of First Baptist Church... hate is here.

As I continue, I remember last night, the excitement (euphoria) of learning Man's Greatest Hospital residents voted 75% in favor of unionizing—I texted a bunch of my friends, and many wrote back, enthused... my high school orchestra friend, a family doctor in Washington State, texted back that residents need to be treated "humanely," and I agree.

I pass the Footlight Club, America's oldest community theater, then the Eliot School, with its sign for Schoolyard Sunday Jazz concerts. Then I cross Jamaicaway and I'm at the pond, and I imagine taking one of the rowboats out....

I bump into my friend's father, a Dana Farber doctor in his 70s. I join him, tell him about our plans to travel to Korea, and my desire to do something biomedical on the trip. Terry's dad tells me of his upcoming family vacation to Georgia, and I recall Kathy's and my wedding at Lullwater, and the Decatur County

Courthouse. Terry is busy with family, doctoring, and looking for a new teaching job, he tells me. And we part ways.

I struggle to do some push-ups on a cross bar, traverse "Crazyway," and soon I'm at First Baptist. They've covered the graffiti with black plastic but it's still visible. It's ironic, because right across the street is the Post Office, which has a sign which describes Jamaica Plain as "The Eden of America," its nickname in the 1800s. An "Eden," an oasis which attracts Neo-Nazis.

I continue through JP, passing Boomerangs, with its blue/orange sign ("Fight AIDS") and stop at my favorite Little Free Library. Today I spot a book, "how to play the Harmonica," and with a loose association it makes me think of Marjorie, my grandmother, who carried a harmonica in her purse...

And now I'm at "Papercuts Bookstore," dreaming of this book, having it on the shelves there, for sale... that would be amazing...

A 39 bus rumbles by, and I walk past the St. Thomas Aquinas Roman Catholic Church, which makes me remember Nanna and Rosary Cathedral in Toledo, and her advice for me to "pray."

Then I'm at the BHA, and I'm transported back to Cincinnati, when I was young, scurrying into Mary Ann's apartment on Williamsburg...

And I come to the Youth Center, its colorful mural, "You are Important," and "Eres Importante."

Yours, Phil

June 10, Saturday, 10:44 AM

Dearest Albert,

John just hit a bloop single then scored when the next hitter smashed one into centerfield! Little League at Johnson Field on a Saturday morning... Now, my son sits near me, dirt on his pants leg from his slide. Our player :)

I lean my foot against the backstop, reclining in my chair, and think back to my 10-mile run this morning through the fog. The run melted away my worries, and for 90 minutes I escaped from my "imprisonment." One idea that came to me was the importance of "proving myself to be healthy and sane..."

Proving myself to others and to me. I've been through so much, and running marathons, writing a book, and creating videos provides a timestamp of normalcy. I can run, write something cogent, create something praiseworthy. A video is the ultimate "proof" in this modern world; in a video, the impression is recorded, as we battle stereotypes of people with bipolar.

Yours, Phil

June 12, Monday, 6:51 AM

Dearest Albert,

Here I am, focused on my DDD, after months of writing, and now I have Zeke from the UMass MFA program to help "coach" me. Onward!

John is coughing, Oma is emptying the dishwasher, and Margo is sitting calmly. Kathy comes over to the couch and sits next to me—our arms touching, even though I'm sweaty post-run. We kiss; she giggles like a teenager. Ah, love.

"We've been living here for more than 5 years," she says, sipping coffee. "I can't believe it." She yawns, rubs her eyes, pushes off my knee and stands, opens the curtains... we've been married 10 years... it seems like our wedding was yesterday. And the day that we met, at the UCSD Medical Center in 2009... also yesterday.

She stands by the front window, looking out at her garden,

black sleeveless shirt, green shorts, mismatched flip flops. Sniffles. Still cute—beautiful.

Yours, Phil

June 13, Tuesday, 6:57 AM

Dearest Albert,

Margo is licking her legs, grooming herself. Probably it's soothing. I sit, finally having caught my breath after a sprint this morning with Gary/Pablo. A sprint for me; a saunter for them. But I kept up. Mental toughness. And I hear the morning birds outside and think of the idea I had yesterday—"Zen and the Art of Birdwatching." It's not motorcycle maintenance, but it's more natural. Observing. Learning their patterns.

It makes me think of yesterday's clinic at Malcolm X. I have several categories of patients—men with chronic back pain, on disability / unemployed; Cape Verdean women, usually working at the North Coast Fish Factory or as a hotel housekeeper, with fibromyalgia; Dominican men who drive Uber/Lyft. And another broad category—the openly anxious/afraid—of what? Sickness, death, penury? I try to soothe them.

Yours, Phil

June 14, Wednesday, 6:44 AM

Dearest Albert,

First, a memory—1998, and I was interviewing for combined BA/MD 8 year programs, and was accepted into "GEMS," Guaranteed Entrance into Medical School at the University of Louisville. But I turned it down and went to Brown University. My parents stayed in Lexington and I moved to Rhode Island.

But now I'm imagining a different scenario—say 10 years from now John is accepted to UCLA (or wherever, far away). I'm 52;

Kathy is 60. Will we stay in Boston while our only child moves 3000 miles away? Or would we migrate somehow, follow him, rent a small apartment for ourselves?

What if in an alternate universe, my father had retired from UK or gotten a faculty job at the University of Rhode Island, and my mom a nursing job at Hospice of Providence and they had followed me to the Ocean State, still available for dinner on weekends? Maybe they would've lived in a little cabin in Scituate, while I studied on College Hill.

The hypothetical question is how to keep our family together when kids are growing up?

I could have gone to GEMS for 8 years, came home to Lexington on the weekends for Cincinnati Chili.

But my eyes were opened by my experiences at Brown. Going there was a good decision.

Were my parents lonely when their only child moved 700 miles from home? Yes. But they kept busy with work, hobbies, etc, and I don't recall them trying to keep me nearby.

Margo kicks me. "Oww," I yelp.

Change of subject—I would love to lose a bit of these love handles. Running doesn't hurt, but it doesn't solve the problem. Maybe if I ran 10 miles a day instead of 4; or wasn't on aripiprazole/ lithium; or ate spinach more.

Margo's nails tap against the floor.

Oma kisses the dog's head and the two of them walk back to the kitchen.

"You already had breakfast," she says.

Back to GEMS—my idea is to be non-judgmental. I chose to go to college in Rhode Island; my parents chose to remain in Kentucky.

Yours, Phil

June 15, Thursday, 7:01 AM

Dearest Albert,

Cannibalism!

That was a topic of discussion on this morning's run because of Cormac McCarthy's recent death. Is the fear of being eaten by other humans a driving force in life?

Or are we more afraid of being devoured by lions, tigers?

Evolutionarily speaking it seems anxiety developed to help protect us from these dangers.

But now "we" are petrified of people different from "us"—Republican rednecks with their AR-15s; or Russians/ North Koreans/ Chinese / Iranians / Palestinians, who are demonized; or immigrants; or black people. Danger, danger. But maybe "we" should be more afraid of middle class white liberals?

The real "cannibals?" I don't know.

—

Yesterday in the clinic, I saw a patient I knew well, a young woman with cirrhosis who was declining, so I sent her to the hospital. It reminded me of the Phil Ochs song, "There But for Fortune."

All of us who are healthy, and whose family members are healthy, are lucky. To be grateful; to strive for better health for all, is important.

Yours, Phil

June 16, Friday, 5:25 AM

Dearest Albert,

Last night I had a patient from Ukraine, perhaps my first ever. The reason for the visit was chronic pain, but I was thinking about the impact of the *war* on my patient's symptoms. When your country is torn apart, how does that impact your carpal tunnel? Suffering is complicated, and has to do with entrapment of the median nerve, but also imprisonment of millions as bombs are dropped. A steroid injection might help with the pain, but the suffering? Why do humans keep bombing?

Margo's eyes flutter—half asleep, half awake, tail touching her jaw.

Yours, Phil

And 11:02 AM

I'm on hold for 30 minutes, trying to help a patient get an appointment with a surgeon (who probably makes >$1 million/year). The patient only speaks Spanish and the appointment was never scheduled. I listen to the soft jazz, look at MEGA, sigh.

"Desculpa, es importante que hacemos este cita," I say. (I'm sorry, it's important we make this appointment).

But patients are backing up.

June 18, Sunday, 11:17 AM

Dearest Albert,

It's a drizzly Father's Day and I'm walking Margo past the garden. The rain picks up, and we pause under a tree. I think of the Globe front page article I was reading about the failing Jeremiah Burke High School. I sigh. The public schools are so troubled, while the rich flee to private academies...

A bumble bee flies by us, and heads toward the peas, the corn, the beans.

I briefly say hello to a neighbor who is vacuuming out the trunk of her car.

Her husband climbs on a bike and attaches their dog to the handlebars. He rides, helmet-less, down Santa Rosa, the dog bounding next to him. Margo sees them, and starts barking wildly and pulling.

I think of JP—good community, but we could have more friendships, support, etc.

Margo and I come out of the rain and settle on our couch. I put on Alejandro Fernandez.

Yours, Phil

And 7:51 PM

For Father's Day we had a nice dinner of Cincinnati Chili, but I'm unhappy. My patient on 270 MME of oxycodone sent me several messages. He had asked for 7 extra days of opioids, but I didn't comply.

It's upsetting—our whole health system is fucked up. Chronic pain is a good example. The Sacklers get away with murder, but those of us in primary care are forced to keep prescribing high doses. It's difficult to taper these patients, or even to get them referred to pain medicine. I didn't write the original prescription!

Margo knows I'm upset, and sits close to me on the couch.

Oma and John listen to a baseball documentary in the other room.

At least things are better than Father's Day 2020, when I was locked up on the inpatient psych ward at Man's Greatest Hospital, and the psychiatrist wouldn't discharge me to see my son.

Repeat—you are free. You are home with your family. May you be well. May everyone be well.

Yours, Phil

June 19, Monday, 10:46 AM

Dearest Albert,

Too many patients; they are backing up. 11 on the schedule so far, and Lester just handed me another face-sheet. Another rash. A 69-year-old woman with diabetes. Being an urgent care doc means you are abused by the system. I dive back into the fire. The hamster wheel is where I'm going to be for the next 3 hours, my white coat trailing behind me as I race from room to room, log in MEGA, log out of MEGA.

Yours, Phil

And then, 5:43 PM

A sunny afternoon, at the English High School track, the long jump. John goes down the straightaway, takes a leap, into the sandpit. And he dives—a world record!

"My hands touched the ground first," he says. "That's where I won the record."

Another attempt, and he lands, feet first. A great Juneteenth. And now, we're doing a pickle, baseball in the long jump pit.

I'm wanting to stay forever.

But I find myself at home. John is talking about getting drafted and going to the majors, or maybe going to college instead. It's dinnertime—red lentil soup.

June 20, Tuesday, 7:17 AM

Dearest Albert,

I'm relieving memories of my 2003 Literature and Medicine course at Brown with Professor Arnold Weinstein. Among many other books/essays, we read "My Own Country," about AIDS in rural Tennessee, and got to meet the author, Dr. Abraham Verghese, who has become a role model for me, a storyteller-physician.

Yesterday in clinic I saw "Jane," a youngish patient who complained of abdominal discomfort, and heartburn. It turned out this had first occurred after some drinking and vomiting. I asked her about bulimia, and she said this had never happened before. I found myself speaking awkwardly.

I say this as someone who feels like he has a degree of binge eating disorder. Even last night, I fell asleep at 9 pm, but awakened at 10 and found myself with a bowl of granola. Not an enormous amount of food, and I never had self-induced vomiting, but this eating was bothersome.

Mostly I blame the aripiprazole and lithium, but also to be fair I used to eat cereal at night years ago, long before I was diagnosed with bipolar. So maybe it's just a habit.

Jane, yesterday's patient with the abdominal discomfort, told me she gets full from eating a half banana, and worries if something is wrong. I agreed to her request for a gastroenterology consult, even though the chance of a Mallory-Weiss tear was remote. What I wanted to recommend was a behavioral health consult.

I yawn. Margo snores, shifts in her sleep. I think back to Professor Weinstein's course. Here I am, 20 years later, trying to tell my own stories.

Yours, Phil

4

Summer

June 21, Wednesday, 4:39 PM
Dearest Albert,
John is watching baseball and I'm thinking about food. Clearly my plan for weight loss isn't working—even though I'm running, my weight remains in the 190s.

I spoke today to Fats, my nutritionist at Man's Greatest Hospital, and we decided on a different approach. Until our next visit I'm going to keep a "mindful eating journal."

For instance, right now, I'm not hungry, but it is 4:40 PM so I'm thinking about food—a banana, perhaps? I'm still feeling a touch of residual nausea—this morning I woke up and promptly vomited—this seldom happens to me. I called in sick to work, because I felt weak, with chills. After some rest I'm a little better. I look in the freezer—frozen samosas Kathy bought, appealing. Instead, I take a nectarine from the fridge. I bite it—good.

Yours, Phil

June 22, Thursday, 9:35 AM
Dearest Albert,

I just paid Hannah Folts, my employment lawyer, over $2200 for her ~6 hours of work. $375 per hour, precisely calculated. And where am I?

Sitting with Margo, worrying about my mounting legal bills, and the skills assessment (who knows what will happen with that).

Being a physician dissident is great and all, but I am headed the wrong way financially.

And I have this billing problem with the insurance companies—only MassHealth (Medicaid) agrees to reimburse for my clinical care.

A mess.

Kathy said she would be ok if I leave medicine. I'm only 42 years old, and could do something different.

Mahatma Gandhi became increasingly dissatisfied with the legal profession and eventually turned into an activist.

Margo shifts in her sleep.

I could become a professional dog walker. Margo's yellowish eyes, her brown legs, which transition into white paws.

Yours, Phil

June 23, Friday, 7:21 AM

Dearest Albert,

John just finished reading a book about D-Day and is studying a world atlas on his carpet. "Apa, I want to look at the map with you some more," he says.

I think back to my patient last night, a Central American lady whose son, about John's age, is stuck back home. She is depressed as it is unclear what will happen. Our broken immigration system. I look at John, with his atlas, rolling on the floor, and remember her in the Malcolm Xexam room. Her chest pain, arm pain, emotional anguish. I gave ibuprofen. My bandaids.

"Whatcha think, kid?" I ask.

"Apa, can you believe this area is part of Asia, this area part of Europe, this area part of Asia?" he queries. I want to hold him tight, to protect him from all the badness out there.

A world where parents are separated from children because of their nationality, skin color, language.

Yours, Phil

June 24, Saturday, 1:50 PM

Dearest Albert,

I'm at a union organizing meeting. We have 12 health care workers here and some snacks. Organizing is hard but we are gradually making progress.... It's like we are at mile 1 or 2 of a marathon... how to keep up the energy?

Yours, Phil

June 25, Sunday, 8:40 PM

Dearest Albert,

I'm in the bathtub, trying to recuperate from a busy Sunday. Choro music with my friend Josh, a clarinetist; an 8-year-old's birthday party; going to my mom's; and 3 hours of baseball. I let the water envelop me, like I'm back in the womb. The conflicts are washed away; I'm "baptized" free from stress.

Next week—writing, music, and a digital detox, best I can. Zen, breathing, blowing bubbles. Now I need some toy boats.

Yours, Phil

June 26, Monday, 9:21 AM

Dearest Albert,

I'm in green team, primary care—I just saw a 68-year-old Cape Verdean lady wearing a lovely dress, who was concerned about nutrition. Can she eat eggs, watermelon, sweet potato, and drink milk and coffee? "All in moderation," I told her—a plan for life.

I need to follow my own advice.

Yours, Phil

June 27, Tuesday, 3:41 PM

Dearest Albert,

I just finished the meeting with my bosses at Malcolm X, and a zoom with the associate director at Physician Help Inc. The $15,500 skills assessment—no update. Meanwhile my MEGA Inbasket continues to overflow with calls, results, staff messages, cc'd charts, patient advice requests, scanned documents, outside events, medication cancellations, prior authorizations, referral messages, etc.

One message stands out—it's **Bold**. The patient was terminated from his job because of his vision. He is a 46-year-old man, Cape Verdean Creole speaking, and is trying to access unemployment. One eye isn't working, and the other eye isn't so good, either. "Sure," I'll write you a letter," I tell him with the help of our interpreter.

Sometimes in life you have to use **bold** to get others attention.

Yours, Phil

PS—As I open his chart in MEGA, I say aloud, "why doesn't his fucking millionaire ophthalmologist write this fucking letter?"

June 29, Thursday, 7:00 AM

Dearest Albert,

Yesterday I saw 9 patients in clinic—a whirlwind.

First, a lady from Cape Verde, retired from working in a laundry, with some musculoskeletal complaints.

Second, a man with obesity and hypertension, at high risk for cardiovascular disease.

Third, an older lady with fibromyalgia, who tends to ruminate on her chronic pain, yet is also cheerful at times.

Fourth, a patient with TMJ.

Fifth, a lady with developmental delay, whose MassHealth Contract for Adult Foster Care has expired.

Sixth, a man with proteinuria who needs to see a nephrologist, but it hasn't happened.

Seventh, a patient with a foot injury, his ankle purple and swollen.

Eighth, a woman from Cape Verde, asking for help with the N-648 immigration/citizenship form, a medical exemption from the requirement to learn civics and English.

Ninth, a man, originally from the DR, with blood pressure and cholesterol issues (who also enjoys pickup baseball).

That's just a snapshot of my 3+ hours on the green team in primary care yesterday. I enjoyed it but at one point the hamster wheel / treadmill left me **shaking with stress**, wanting a white coat walkout.

I pet Margo. How to remain Zen, as I advance toward my goal? This seems to be a theme...

Yours, Phil

And, more at 6:56 PM

I am a good doctor at times. Rainbow, one of our nurse practitioners, called me in to see a patient with erythematous, tender nodules on the shins. I recognized this as probable erythema nodosum. My colleague was impressed.

It would be terribly sad to throw away two decades of medical training/ experience. But our health system is toxic. We need Moral Mondays at the Massachusetts State House. Maybe my friend Sandhya would be game, following in the footsteps of Charlie Van der Horst.

July 1, Saturday, about 4:45 PM

Dearest Albert,

We're at Dennis-Yarmouth Regional High School, watching a Cape Cod League baseball game between the Brewster Whitecaps and Yarmouth-Dennis Red Sox. A player knocks a home run to left center.

The pitches snap into the catcher's glove, punctuated by an occasional foul ball or hit. A "Red Sox" player sells raffle tickets; the fans lounge on an incline. Grandma goes for a walk, while Oma, John, and I watch a long ball by a Whitecaps hitter—foul. Vacation.

John munches on triscuits, as Oma goes to buy a hot dog. On the Cape in the heat, we're a million miles from Malcolm X. I remember Charlie, always passionate, giving 110% for health justice. What would he say about this Brave New World— Affirmative Action, Roe v Wade repealed, etc?

But advocacy takes a team. It takes planning—who can help me accomplish Moral Mondays with White Coats at the State House?

The fog starts to roll in, and then the temperature drops. Oma and Grandma chat about our upcoming Korea trip. When could we do the Moral Mondays—in mid August, 6 weeks away?

Yours, Phil

July 2, Sunday, mid-Afternoon, unknown time

Dearest Albert,

We're at Colonial Acres beach; sunny but windy, and John/Oma head into the water. Grandma follows them across the sand, bundled up in a sweatshirt. The beach actually reminds me of Kathy's and my honeymoon in Mozambique, but that's another story.

I also think of a song, from the ending of the Gael Garcia Bernal movie, "Y Tu Mama Tambien," *Si no te hubieras ido seria tan feliz* (If you hadn't left, I'd be so happy).

I believe the female lead character developed cancer, and died—my memory.

Last night we had a fire in our backyard fire pit—the flames lulled me to sleep. This morning I ran 11 miles, then John and I went mini-golfing. We each got a hole-in-one.

Seagulls cry out.

Kathy and John are up to their waists, then go under the waves. Grandma sleeps. I watch the motorboats.

When I was a kid, I had a wave cassette tape which put me to sleep. Crashing waves is one of the most relaxing sounds. Their rhythmic nature.

"Si no te hubieras ido, seria tan feliz."

Yours, Phil

July 3, Monday, 5:27 AM

Dearest Albert,

I know the time, because I'm in our little Yarmouth house, which has a wall clock. The rain woke me; then, the birds helped finish the job. I hope the weather passes, so John will get his morning baseball clinic in with the Cape Cod League college stars.

I left my watch, iPhone, and laptop in Boston, and the impact of minimal technology (Oma's iPhone is still around) is interesting. My wrist is conspicuously empty, for example. I'm not being judgmental, but it's clear I have a habit of repeatedly checking the time, even though time is so artificial.

In modern society we are so glued to our Google Calendars and the idea of timeliness and productivity, we become so stressed out.

And the iPhone! An incredible tool, access to all the world's information, music, memory, friends—but so addictive! How to use this technology so it doesn't use us?

I'm hopeful that my meditation practice will help me.

Yours, Phil

And mid-Afternoon, maybe 2 PM

John heads down to the water [my pen just ran out of ink]—he is collecting stones. Oma and Grandma are sunning themselves.

"That plane is flying so low," John says, looking up to the sky in response to a jet headed toward Hyannis Airport. Then he goes back to playing with his stones.

I study the people—mostly white, young. And I listen to someone's country-rock music. It was jarring to see a man proudly sporting a "TRUMP 2024" camouflage baseball cap a few minutes ago, here in Massachusetts.

I adjust the shelter I'm sitting in, think of my Korean wife, half-Korean son, the anti-Asian sentiment among many in America.

A double kayak passes by us, parallel to shore; a drink of my seltzer water. Tonight to Chatham to watch another Cape Cod League game; tomorrow one more morning baseball clinic at Dennis-Yarmouth High. Then we'll head home, back to iPhones and MEGA. I cover my feet with a towel—they are burning up. Oma and John splash, stop, then start up again. Zen and the art of beach-going. I see Grandma's varicose veins, covered in zinc

paste.
Yours, Phil

July 4, Tuesday, about 9:30 AM (still no watch)
Dearest Albert,

I'm walking the track at Dennis-Yarmouth Regional High while John attends baseball clinic—and I'm in pursuit of Grandma. I catch up to her and we walk a little as the drizzle turns into rain. She tells me she doesn't want a PCA while we are abroad, citing the expense. But I think the real reason is she doesn't want to acknowledge she's in decline. That's becoming clear to Kathy and me, with the colonoscopy incident a few months ago and now, the delusional parasitosis at her apartment.

My mother tells me about the best time of her life, 2014-2019, when she and Grandpa took care of John at Harbor Point....

And then, a rain delay—we take shelter under a wooden stand past the center field fence, while the players run to the dugout. Grandma eats an apple and the rain continues. "Where did the kids go?" She asks, and I tell her. Beetles climb up and down the wooden beams of the structure.

Maybe Oma will come back with an umbrella. But Grandma decides to go for the dugout, and treks across the outfield. I stay put.

Yours, Phil

7:11 PM

Back in Jamaica Plain, outside Gary's house, for his son's birthday party. John is playing soccer with the other boys in the backyard, and Kevin is talking about going to Coney Island and watching a Nathan's Hot Dog eating contest—gluttony.

I find myself feasting on chips and hummus (at least I avoided the pizza), so I start my stopwatch and stop eating. Up to 11 minutes now. How to stop, when eating is so glorified in our culture? Self-control?

I retreat to the car, avoiding the food, and sit behind the wheel and write. I think about the conversations... Kevin advising me about credit card fees when we travel to Seoul; the cost of electricity in Massachusetts (as we install our wall air conditioning units).

Now, with my iPhone on, my watch on, I think of time. It was just yesterday that John was born, and now he's almost 9.

July 5, Wednesday, 8:20 AM
Dearest Albert,
Everything is frustrating. The Malcolm X computers don't turn on. The paperwork. Having 10 patients in 3.5 hours. Liz Lester comes in; we chat about our vacations. She was in Truro, and on the national seashore beaches. Then Julieta arrives; our medical assistant, heavily tattooed, a singer.

I look at the 10 names on my MEGA schedule, then dash off a secure chat message to Gerald Daneeka, another physician at the health center.

Three 30 minute visits; seven 15 minute visits. I breathe—these clinical sessions feel harder than a marathon in terms of stress, and yet we do them so often (I guess my marathon time is about 5:20, so that would be an extra long Malcolm X clinical session).

But the hamster wheel is about to start—seven female patients, three male patients, ages 20-85. And one of our medical assistants isn't here yet—wait, she just arrived.

Being on the time clock, a cog in the machine, the health care industrial complex.

Yours, Phil

July 6, Thursday, 1:27 PM
Dearest Albert,
I study my At-A-Glance planners from 2018 and 2020, looking for clues as to how I can avoid getting sick once again.

2018 was busy, with clinics, consults, parenting, advocacy, etc. We had the hemorrhagic fever situation. And then on June 4th, a similar patient in the ICU, triggered my memories, my fears of a hemorrhagic fever virus.

Over the next couple of weeks my anxiety exploded into mania and culminated on Friday, June 22, 2018, at 4 PM, when I was called in to meet with Dr. Georgia Bush and Dr. Electric Chair (the Chairman of Medicine).

We sat in his office, I was placed on administrative leave, and referred to Physician Help Inc, my brain on fire.

In 2020, the situation was so different, with the COVID pandemic, but eerily similar, with an accelerating nervous energy.

On June 15, 2020 at 5 PM, I talked by video with the university President, recounting my concerns about nosocomial COVID transmission and the danger that health workers faced because of insufficient personal protective equipment.

The next day I was Section 12'd at the Man's Greatest Hospital Emergency Department.

I tried to flee, was chased down by security, captured, and admitted to the inpatient psychiatry ward.

The ED security guards were faster than me.

But could they complete a marathon?

Yours, Phil

July 8, Saturday, 6:20 AM

Dearest Albert,

Shabbat, and I stumble upon a Globe article about an exhibit on prison writers at Harvard's Houghton Library. So I think of you, and take out the brown binder filled with letters you wrote from the Lebanon Correctional Institution from 1971-1972.

I page through them, memories of your incarceration. A half-century ago, and how you used writing, reading, and music to persevere and even thrive, as far as someone can thrive in prison. You learned computer programming, became president of the Jaycees, wrote for the prison newspaper, etc.

Only one letter from your mother survives, from "Thanksgiving Day" (? 1971), of course addressed to "Dearest Al."

In it, "Mom" / my grandmother, Marjorie Lederer, writes of gratitude despite your imprisonment.

"Thanks for all we've learned; and thanks for the composure we have maintained."

Marjorie writes of hope, despite her only son being locked up with murderers.

And you used your letters, about 30 years later, to write your own book, "Leave Not Hope Behind."

I'm using my letters as the basis for this book.

I stretch, yawn, chew on some ice. Vermont departure in <1 hour. My 3rd marathon attempt.

Yours, Phil

July 10, Monday, 6:36 AM

Dearest Albert,

Race report, Vermont's Mad Marathon. Hills and heat make for a tough race. However, at mile 17 I am picked up by one of the pacing groups led by Tom, from Minnesota, who has run

>600 marathons (recently running through metastatic prostate cancer, I learn from Google).

For the next 6+ miles I stick with him and am buoyed by his anecdotes (watermelon!), and am cajoled to run-walk, run-walk. Beginning marathoners, find a pacer!

Now I have some fearsome toe blisters and leg pain but am ok.

Second—keep going with advocacy! I am inspired by Vermont-PNHP President Dr. Betty Keller, who fights for a single payer despite challenges. We need more activists like her.

It's like Eliud Kipchoge says—"it takes a team," and "no human is limited."

Yours, Phil

July 11, Tuesday, 9 AM
Dearest Albert,
Maybe my job isn't so bad, after all.

The plumbers are here fixing our toilet—the grime, rust, paper towels; bending over to screw in bolts, the leaks, cracked porcelain. Their job is bad on the back, the knees; and the diet—plumbers are all obese, from what I've seen.

They carry out the old, cracked toilet; bring in the new, shiny one. The banging noises, their guttural conversation; blue uniforms; vans parked outside. "I got the caps here," one says. Both are white, one in his 30s, the other in his 50s. "Sorry to bother you, sir; you got any more paper towels?" the older man mumbles.

I spy on them from the kitchen. But I can't make out their conversation, just the older one laughing. The younger man picks up the new toilet, sets it in place.

I wonder about these men—are they unionized?

Last night we had our card signing on Zoom. Will we be able

to organize Malcolm X?

I hear running water. "You know why it was rocking' and rollin'?" he asks me. And he explains the problem.

Yours, Phil

12:44 PM

Tom was an angel, sent to help me cross the finish line. I've met several angels in life. Ioana Bica. Hamza Brimah. Elizabete Nunes. It's not common, but it occurs—people collide, exchange energy, a word, a handshake. An encounter which propels you in a different direction.

Dr. Fanon said the "Angel" was the signifier from today's psychoanalysis session. It reminds me of my mother, with her discussions of Guardian Angels when I was a kid. And Nanna.

Angels, spirits, ghosts, shamans—is that what a physician should be talking about? Better to stick to something more benign, like meditation/ mindfulness?

I'm here at Malcolm X, feeling the stress, but I'll keep my ears and eyes open for Angels in unlikely places.

July 12, Wednesday 6:47 AM

Dearest Albert,

It's gonna be a scorcher, I can tell. Margo and I walked and the sun was attacking us.

"Can I see who won the ASG?" John asks. "Yeah," I say, and he heads to the computer. The newspaper hasn't arrived. It seems to come about 60% of the days.

Margo walks over and whiskers me so I take off her harness. She's collared but a bit more liberated. John is still in the office, presumably reading about the heroics of the National League or American League players during the All Star Game last night.

I think of my emotional and intellectual sprint today. 3.5

Hours. 11 patients, 1 by telemedicine. Diabetics, chronic pain, a man with a recent STEMI (heart attack). I've prepared for clinic as best I can, but still, these 15 minute visits. I'm a broken record.

Margo sits by the front door in the sun.

Yours, Phil

July 14, 7:06 AM

Dearest Albert,

I sit at the living room table, which is covered by a half-finished jigsaw puzzle of the MBTA. The train lines are completed, but the outlying neighborhoods are not. A stack of mostly white pieces, some with light blue, others with word fragments or short purple lines (commuter rail).

I turn off the air conditioner. Yawn. Look toward John's open door, see some legs.

The rain has let up—that's good, although I like how it keeps down the heat.

I put my index finger in my left ear, wiggle back and forth.

I hear Oma—"What would you like for breakfast? Oatmeal? Granola with yogurt?" Their voices are quiet. Laughter.

I straighten my papers. Turn back on the AC. Oma measures John's height—he's growing like a sunflower.

Yours, Phil

July 15, Saturday, 2:55 AM

Dearest Albert,

I'm in the middle of a union meeting. Elana Sawyer, head of human resources, sent out an email saying Malcolm X Health Center thinks unionization is the wrong direction.

It's like the old song, "which side are you on?"

Are you with the union, or not?

We're making progress, and I think we can win—but it's all hands on deck.

We need to get people militant, activated. Everyone can help us advance, win over hearts and minds.

Yours, Phil

July 16, Sunday 8:10 PM

Dear Al,

I changed my violin strings today, the first time in a year. And John and I went running in the rain around Jamaica Pond. And we played ping pong on our dining room table. The kid is good.

I phoned my friend Pluto, in California—he says I ought to be funnier in my videos. I'm too serious. Maybe I'll try ventriloquy.

The blisters on my toes from the Vermont marathon are finally healing.

Yours, Phil

July 17, Monday, 9:01 PM

Dearest Albert,

Kathy purchased a refrigerator lock today. We'll see if it helps me lose weight—no more snacking.

I saw my primary care doctor today (for 12 minutes) and tomorrow I see my psychiatrist in person. First time since COVID.

I remain upset about the Lithium and Aripiprazole (lack of convincing evidence regarding efficacy; concerns regarding safety). But it's complicated, given my saga with the medical board.

All I can try to do is be kind to myself—it ain't easy, particularly when we're talking about body image and self-acceptance.

Yours, Phil

July 18, 6:59 AM, Tuesday
Dear Al,
Regarding my 9:30 AM appointment with Dr. Roy G. Basch, I'm grateful for his steadfast presence, and I do believe pharmacotherapy is helping me—the question is how much. I'm concerned about my weight, blood pressure, and kidney function. If I were my own doctor—admittedly a bad idea—I would want to be on a lower dose of lithium, because that might reduce the risk of chronic kidney disease.

Do I have science to back this up? Only a systematic review which looked at a few studies and concluded a lower level might be reasonable. But this is unknown.

It's the risks of mania/depression vs potential long term benefits—the Art of medicine. What about the opposite argument—raise the lithium dose—push for a level of 1.0, for example. Is there solid science backing up that argument? Systematic reviews, randomized trials? I think not. So it's snake oil, voodoo.

Yours, Phil

July 21, Friday, 7:16 PM
Dearest Albert,
Oma and John are playing ping-pong on the dining room table. Margo is relaxing.

Ping pong was one of my favorite activities growing up—with Nanna and Babe Cohen, among others. I think it's good for the mind, body, and spirit—it requires quick reflexes, and there's always a lot of laughter. I think ping-pong is a solid anxiolytic and anti-depressant, probably as good as an SSRI, if only we had a randomized trial...

I'm good—not a professional table tennis player, but decent.

Last night I saw a depressed, lonely patient—food stamps aren't enough, so she's always hungry. She's not far from suicide, and only seems to be hanging on for her dog as she struggles to pay her rent, and electricity bill. She's lost weight and has nausea, vomiting.

Our ping pong game continues.

Yours, Phil

July 23, Sunday, 7:30 PM

Dearest Al,

We put a scotch tape "box" on each side of the ping pong table, a target to hit to improve our accuracy. So now our ping-pong games are full of each player saying "In" or "Out," if the serve or rally is hit inside the square—it's kind of like having 2 home plates on the ping pong table. Our rallies are longer, with fewer unforced errors.

Today was good. We went for a family walk; later, Ben Benson came over to play banjo/fiddle on the front porch. Then Oma and I had a long talk about finances, travel, John's school, etc. Now the ping pong. But...

I'm concerned about the Boston Public Schools. One of John's classmates had a big issue with anger and sometimes hit the other kids. The school also has apparently had problems with bullying. Would it be better in a suburban public school or a private school?

And guns are everywhere. We parents ought to be in the streets, demanding better, safer schools.

Yours, Phil

July 24, Monday 7:40 AM
Dearest Albert,
Another week is underway, and I'm a little jealous of Margo. No stress. Just sleep, eat, walk, rest. I've got this pending skills assessment, MEGA notes, unionization, typing up my book. Getting a new workplace monitor since Angel Putzel has resigned. Staying healthy.

Life is like a game of ping pong. You try to keep the ball on the table. Deal with concerns about school. Find a dog sitter. Fix the hole in the bathroom ceiling. Live mindfully. The "ball" ricochets back and forth. You never know what's gonna happen.

John sits next to me, talking baseball. I think of the lonely patient I wrote about last Friday, who was struggling to pay the rent. "There but for Fortune." I look at John, Margo, Oma.

Yours, Phil

PS - 12:33 PM.

I just did 30 minutes of meditation—the most in a long time. I had put 12-1 PM on my calendar as planning for Moral Mondays at the State House, but realized most important is that I experience spiritual growth. What I noticed during the meditation was the distractions—the vacuum cleaner upstairs. And how I tried to reorient from the noises.

I need stability in my life. The opposite of bipolarity. If I have any hope of being "cured" from bipolar in my lifetime, I must become calmer.

If I want to become more "compelling" as a person, to be more "influential," I must change. I visualize being at the State House in late September, say, wearing white coats. Can I remain calm in such a situation? And not fall down the rabbit hole I experienced during the mania of 2018?

More meditation is needed.

July 27, Thursday, 10:11 AM

Dearest Albert,

Sinead O'Connor is dead. I remember my mom talking about her when I was a kid—we enjoyed a Chieftains album, "The Long Black Veil," that she appeared on—the song was "The Foggy Dew."

I wasn't a big fan of her music but I recognize the rebellious Irish Catholic in her and in myself.

Plus, apparently Sinead carried a diagnosis of bipolar.

Deep breath. We shall overcome, if we come together as the Beloved Community.

I need to be tough, kind, and keep working hard. Last night John and I went to a 3 on 3 hockey game at BU—it reminded me of the Kung Fu Gophers team 20 years ago, but much better.

I think of ice hockey as a metaphor for life. It's a ultimate team sport—and you have to be resilient.

Yours, Phil

July 28, Friday, 8:52 PM

Dearest Albert,

I'm exhausted. The heat was oppressive today. John was sick. Morning clinic—URIs, herpes scares.

Meeting with my new boss.

And video editing.

My great toe (marathon) blister is still bugging me.

I posted "My Story," a video about my experience with bipolar, on YouTube.

Now it's time to rest.

I brought a book of short stories, "The Flounder," so maybe I'll relax with that.

The AC is cranking and the fan is spinning.

Yours, Phil

July 29, Saturday, 3:17 PM
Dearest Albert,
Back from the pool. I saw a poster in the hallway that Les Miserables is showing at Milton High.
I watched it about 30 years ago in Detroit, and loved it—the protagonist, Jean Valjean, an escaped prisoner, fighting off the police inspector Javert.
"I'm the stronger man by far, my race is not yet run!" I recall him singing.
–

I did a 5K this morning and recorded a bit of video too, before and after. And regarding my big race, October 1st—the Minneapolis Marathon—I just need an airplane ticket.
And assuming I'm not on call, I think I'll sign up for the Manchester, New Hampshire marathon—November 12.
But back to the present—Bread Day at Grandma's. She's reading "The Book Woman of Troublesome Creek"—about a 1930s era librarian in Kentucky.
We're far from the Bluegrass state, but we have memories of our old Kentucky home, 2072 Oleander Drive.
Yours, Phil

July 30, 7:33 PM, Sunday
Dearest Albert,
Kathy and I are squabbling. She was telling John about various private schools he might apply to, even after I asked her to please stop.
The situation at the Boston Public Schools is frustrating. His school is ok, but in general the district is crappy, because parents

with resources flee to the private schools or public schools in the suburbs. All the options are infuriating. And I'm upset with the societal apathy around our schools.

We don't fight for better urban public schools. We give up and start down the route of the privates, which we don't really want. Are we people of conscience?

I would like to talk with my neighbor, Mark, before we get too far down this path—he teaches at one of the local private schools. Perhaps I am overreacting.

Yours, Phil

July 31, Monday, 8:24 PM

Dearest Albert,

More ping pong tonight—good rallies by John, Oma, myself.

Then Oma was practicing Moonlight Sonata—Beethoven—on piano. A nice night.

Yours, Phil

August 1, Tuesday, 7:41 AM

Dearest Albert,

I didn't sleep great—being on call does that to me. And I'm paranoid about sleep disturbance, given my bipolar. Anyway, I'm ok.

Now I'm listening to Ella Jenkins, a record, as Margo wanders over.

John lounges on the couch, and I think about today. Probably I have 60 "low key" minutes to type up my book. Yesterday I made progress. If I focus, I can get closer to printing out a first draft. "Low-key" minutes means no stress, just trying to get into a flow state.

Yours, Phil

PS– 5 PM

I find my flow state at Curtis Hall, floating on my back in the swimming pool, admiring the paint on the ceiling. Then diving, surrounded by bubbles.

August 4, Friday, 4:01 PM

Dearest Albert,

I just deleted YouTube from my phone.

Yours, Phil

August 5, Saturday, 8:37 AM

Dearest Albert,

Saturday morning clinic. Awaiting my first of 11 patients (I could have more), feeling the stress of working in a sweatshop; trying to stay Zen.

Yours, Phil

And 12:32 PM

Dan Masters, my patient, is dead. He had an addiction problem, as well as depression.

August 6, Sunday, 7:16 PM

Dearest Albert,

After a Red Sox game at Fenway with John, attempting to adopt the optimistic Costa Rican mindset (our friends just got back). Pura Vida!

Yours, Phil

August 7, Monday, 9:43 AM

Dearest Al,

I'm trying to maintain "Pura Vida," but Dr. Roach's latest report to the medical board made me angry. It's a power struggle

for the future of Malcolm X—and I'm with the union. I'll discuss with Dr. Erin Beck.
Pura vida,
Phil

August 8, Tuesday, 7:49 AM
Dearest Albert,
John and Oma are getting ready to go—soccer camp, and clinic. Margo and I stay behind. "Have Fun," I call out.
Yours,
Phil

August 9, Wednesday, 8:27 AM
Dearest Al,
In clinic—about to get started… breathe…
Yours, Phil

August 10, Thursday, 4:08 PM
Dearest Albert,
Getting ready for work…. More MEGA… we'll see how this evening goes—MEGA. I'm missing the good old days of paper charts.
Yours, Phil

August 11, Friday, 7:11 AM
Dearest Albert,
TGIF. I'm on the couch with Margo after a run. Caked in sweat. Thinking about Malcolm X, trying to stay calm like Margo, but getting jazzed up. Agitated. Do my "physiologic sigh," Andrew Huberman's double in-breath, then one out-breath. I start to drift off. Footsteps upstairs, the 2-year-old running around.

Sunlight, on the closet door, the hardwood floor. Margo extends her paws into me, as if she's offering a hug. She sighs.

I hear Oma cleaning out a dish in the kitchen; John shuffling around in his bedroom.

Yours, Phil

August 12, Saturday, 3:50 PM

Dearest Al,

We're at Grandma's, planning a schedule of zoom calls for when we go to South Korea. It's a 13-hour time difference. We leave in one week!

Yours, Phil

August 14, Monday, 8:47 PM

Dearest Al,

We're getting closer and closer to Seoul; everyone is excited; Oma's been stressed, but we'll get through it.

Yours, Phil

August 15, Tuesday, 6:44 AM

Dearest Albert,

Yesterday, John refused to go basketball camp, saying the coach is "harsh," and if you miss a shot you have to "do five push-ups." It threw us into a frenzy, but we improvised. We actually had a great day—he and I went to Juicy Greens, then the pool at Curtis Hall—he's becoming a better swimmer.

I feel something between Oma and I—perhaps it's stress. Work, home, travel, etc.

We're up to 155 signatures on the union cards. It's good.

This morning we ran in the rain—Suz's mom has breast cancer.

Yours, Phil

August 16, Wednesday, 3:57 PM

Dearest Albert,

John is on the computer, looking at soccer players. Oma is doing a zoom interview. I'm flossing.

The big news is Dr. Jo Roach is resigning from Malcolm X. She didn't give a reason.

And I binge ate some triscuits. And we're 3 days until South Korea.

See if I can get my book to the UMass MFA student, Zeke.

Yours, Phil

August 17, Thursday, 3:57 PM

Dearest Albert,

Wayharmoni and Oma are talking in Korean; John is in his room; Margo is snoozing. I'm on the couch.

Oma tells me her mom is excited by the baby cardinals outside the dining room window—they are almost big enough to fly away. I hear them squeaking.

"Ka-ja," Oma calls out. [Let's go!]

Yours, Phil

August 18, Friday, 7:16 AM

Dearest Al,

Last night clinic was busy, but good—I had a patient from East Africa, which reminded me of our time in Mozambique. I once had a friend who was from Pemba. She and her husband were so friendly to us, having us over to their home several times. But we lost touch, ten years ago. I wonder how they are.

Yours, Phil

SUMMER

August 20, Sunday, 8:42 PM

Dearest Al,

It's been a tiring couple of days—Wayharmoni was vomiting so we went from the Logan Airport terminal to Faulkner Hospital. She's ok now, and we are trying to rebook our flight to Korea. Patience.

Yours, Phil

August 21, Monday, 4:40 PM

Dearest Albert,

I just saw a "coy," a big orange fish, while kayaking around Jamaica Pond. I also saw dragonflies and a large brown bird— kind of like a pelican (?). It was so peaceful on the water, I made up a song:

Row, row, row my kayak
Across Jamaica Pond
Merrily, merrily, merrily, merrily
Dip my magic wand

Anyway, the healing power of nature wowed me. And at 7 AM we will fly to Seattle, then Seoul.

I'll be looking for as much wilderness as possible during our South Korea journey.

All my worries of Malcolm X and the medical board will be left behind.

This trip is about spending time with John, Oma, Wayharmoni— and creating some memories.

And then, back home to Jamaica Pond.

Yours, Phil

August 22, Tuesday, 6:51 AM, Seattle time, 30,000 feet

Dearest Al,

We're winging it towards Washington State and I'm listening to Buddy Thomas, the fiddler. I'm thinking about self-compassion.

Life can be hard, and I want to be my own friend.

Whether it comes to my body image, my job, or stress from the medical board, I've learned about the importance of just being present with myself.

My friend I-Jun sent me a booklet about Korean Buddhism and it makes me think about acceptance.

Yours, Phil

August 25, Friday, 11:57 AM, South Korea

Dearest Al,

We're sitting in a cafe near Seoul's City Hall... blueberry milkshakes and ice cream with mung bean. I vomited this morning, maybe from jet lag, but now seem to be doing better.... What can I say? A lot of cars, trains, busses, people—hard for me to focus on mindfulness. It's like Woody Allen said, "sex and death" (I think I'm remembering his movie "Love and Death.")

We're a few miles from Pyongyang with its nuclear weapons, as well as American ones in submarines offshore, but people are going along with their day-to-day routines as if we aren't on the verge of Armageddon.

I try to help Greater Boston Physicians for Social Responsibility, forwarding an email to the assistant of U.S. Representative Stephen Lynch, asking for his leadership on the abolition of nukes. Lynch's office has been minimally responsive—and he's better than some of the other U.S. representatives. What does it take to get some leaders who prioritize peace?

Yours, Phil

August 26, Saturday, 11:33 AM
Dearest Al,
I'm outside our Seoul hotel; we leave for Chongju soon. This morning I had a good 11 mile run-walk to the Han River and along its bike path. I saw a motorboat pulling a water skier and a sign warning me of snakes in the shrubbery. I made it home fine, and we now plan to go visit the DMZ next week.

The question is if I could follow Jim Muller's path and find other physicians (USA, South Korea, North Korea) interested in peace but who would start with a medical education partnership?

For example collaborating to reduce tobacco use in America and the Koreas, or salt/exercise/ hypertension/ obesity, or even tuberculosis? Once we established this partnership, we could move on to advocacy around nuclear weapons, and peace between North and South Korea and America. A pipe dream, sure, but why not dream?

Yours, Phil

August 27, Sunday, 7:56 AM
Dearest Al,
Breathe.
John is watching a Red Sox-Dodgers simulcast on Oma's iPhone. I'm experiencing irritation.
"I want Jansen to come in," he says to himself. "I'm fine with either a home run or a strikeout."
Breathe.
My self-worth is not dependent on my son's screen time.
I can try to influence others, but I cannot control them.
I walk to the hotel room window and look out at the Cheongju skyline.
Yours, Phil

August 28, Monday, 5:36 AM

Dearest Al,

Yesterday we ate the most delicious green grapes, purchased outside Cheongju at a roadside stand near South Korea's "Camp David." We had a nice time visiting with Oma's cousins and other relatives and I brought a handmade drum for 100,000 won. It's used in Salmunori music. But the best part was watching "Uncle John" run around with his nieces and nephews who are around his age. It reminded me of an essay from JAMA, "A Piece of My Mind" by a doctor with cancer, who just wanted to watch his kids play.

I'm going off for a run to ponder the world of "Jew-bus," Jewish Buddhists. I feel an affinity with those folks.

Yours, Phil (Jew-bu?)

August 29, Tuesday, 11:56 AM

Dearest Al,

We're at Seoul's children's science museum and John is playing a game where he rolls a metal ball down an incline and tries to get it through a series of xylophone-like objects into a goal.

Oma is reading something on her phone.

I'm daydreaming about moving to Seoul for a sabbatical. We'd learn Korean, write, and do some health work, along with advocacy for peace on the Korean Peninsula.

Yours, Phil

August 30, Wednesday, 8:58 AM

Dearest Al,

John is laying on our bed, singing "Eye of the Tiger," his favorite baseball song. The washing machine spins behind me.

My phone dings. A final sip of coffee. Korea.
Yours, Phil

August 31, Thursday, 9:03 AM
Dearest Al,
Last night you came to me in a dream—Malcolm X Health Center was demanding a meeting with me on a Thursday morning and I was reluctant to go in because I was off work. You told me they were going to be firing me.
Dream interpretation?
Time to go out on the town—Oma is calling me.
Yours, Phil

September 1, Friday, 9:15 AM
Dearest Al,
We're almost to the end of our Korean sojourn. It's been a great trip—not totally easy, but good. My Korean improved a bit, and I did a lot of daydreaming about a 1-2 year sabbatical. (But Kathy and I haven't discussed it and I doubt she'd be on board).
Yesterday I had lunch with a Korean-American friend a couple of miles away at a traditional restaurant. The last time I saw him was in Addis Ababa, Ethiopia in 2012. He is a neurosurgeon and public health professional with an interest in North Korea—he's made many trips there.
The bottom line about Pyongyang is the 70-year-old war is the biggest public health threat the Koreans, and all of us, face.
Nukes on hair trigger alert with tensions high on the Korean Peninsula, and a new cold war with China and Russia?
President Dwight Eisenhower was right. The military-industrial complex puts us in peril. Back in Boston I could get

active in Mass Peace Action. But how to promote nonviolence?
I'll sing the "Eye of the Tiger," as I proceed.
Yours, Phil

September 2, Saturday, 5:57 PM
Dearest Al,
This will be my last letter from South Korea. I'm at Incheon International Airport in Seoul waiting for Oma, John, and Wayharmoni as they exchange their Won back to dollars.
What can I say about our trip to Korea? In Seoul, everywhere I turned, I saw Namsan, the imposing mountain in the center of the city. And the other orientation point was Hangang, the Han River.
Trees and water, nature helps keep me in balance.
Yours, Phil

September 3, Sunday, 8:33 PM
Dearest Al,
We're home! I'm on the cough with Margo. I miss Korea, and would love to go back and live there someday, but not today.
And tomorrow I'll be running with Gary at 6 AM.
Yours, Phil

September 4, Monday, 7:04 PM
Dearest Al,
John and I are back from baseball with Balazs, Mike, David, and their kids. Oma and Wayharmoni are snoozing, jet lagged. John is reading a Matt Christopher book and I'm trying to relax. For some reason, our visit to my mom's made me feel sad. She was struggling with anxiety and it was hard to see her in that state. Maybe I should look for a support group for

family members of elders with dementia. At least my mom and Wayharmoni got to spend time together :)

They met about twelve years ago and are close, despite the cultural and language gulf.

I think my other worries are about my friend Danny, who is depressed; and, going back to work at Malcolm X. Maybe I should give Monica Potts a call to get the scoop on what's going on? The Boston City Council issued a proclamation in favor of the Malcolm X unionization effort while we were in Seoul. She's been pushing really hard for the union, and despite intimidation from management, we are making progress.

Yours, Phil

September 5, Tuesday, 6:56 AM

Dearest Al,

I'm back from a brisk run with Pablo; John is dressed up in his full catcher's gear, including his new catcher's glove. It's a comedy :)

This kid has passion for baseball.... We finish our game, and he unsnaps his protective vest. I love this boy.

Today I told Pablo I think life is a balance between the "Prizefighter's mentality," a boxer who keeps going, with mental toughness; and a compassionate, zen-like approach to life.

Sometimes we need to race forward, fists up, like our hunter gatherer ancestors closing in on a wounded antelope.

But often, we need compassion and empathy. There is far too much demonization of the "other side" in this world—from North and South Korea to Israel and Palestine, etc.

In retrospect, I learned both the boxer's mentality and the compassionate approach when I was a child.

Yours, Phil

September 6, Wednesday, 7:03 AM

Dearest Al,

John is telling me about the upcoming MLB playoffs; Margo is staring out the door; Oma is gardening. I'm getting ready, mentally, for morning clinic. Eleven patients.

Yours, Phil

September 7, Thursday, 10:36 AM

Dearest Al,

I'm on the 34 bus on my way to boxing. The engine is loud! We pass Leonardo's Barber Shop, which seems to be closed through mid-October. I look around the bus at the other passengers. Almost all are women. We inch up a hill, then idle to let folks off and on. Outside, it's a scorcher.

We pass a U.S. Army "Career Center." My tax dollars at work, just like the Yongsun U.S. Army Base that I kept passing on my daily runs through Seoul.

Yours, Phil

September 8, Friday, 10:59 AM

Dearest Al,

I just saw a young Cape Verdean man for earwax—the encounter made me want to pause and reflect on why I became a physician.

In 1998 I had developed gallstone pancreatitis after rapid weight loss. I required a laparoscopic cholecystectomy and the experience was an ordeal, but it made me interested in medicine. In 2000, I started a Musicians in Hospitals volunteer program in Rhode Island: I felt like the music was healing for some patients. In 2002 I shadowed Dr. Hamza Brimah in Greenwood, Mississippi, the only HIV doctor in the region. 21 years later, despite a diagnosis of bipolar disorder I am still a practicing physician. That in and of itself is remarkable.

Yours, Phil

September 10, Sunday, 2:31 PM

Dearest Al,

We're at Grandma's, on the futon, keeping with the theme of pausing/reflexion. Oma/John had a bit of a tiff this afternoon but we've gotten through it. Now John is having me make up baseball swings for an imaginary baseball lineup.

Yours, Phil

September 11, Monday, 7:23 AM

Dearest Al,

I'm thinking about trash after walking Margo this morning. I picked up some plastic on the street and put it in our recycling bin; today is trash day. We must protect this planet.

Yours, Phil

September 12, Tuesday, 7:26 AM

Dearest Al,

Oma and John just finished a game of ping pong, and Margo is roaming around making high pitched noises. It's funny, but I've found that when one of us gets grumpy or anxious, a game of table tennis can turn things right around. The healing properties of racket sports.

What's worrying me—MEGA, and the medical board, and emotions that bubble up—in myself, Kathy, John, my mom, etc.

Yesterday, I went down to Fuller Village and had tea with my mom, before my violin lesson with Bob Parker. It was nice to see her, even if she was anxious and having problems speaking.

At Bob's we worked on groove and "pocket"—i.e. rhythm—danceability—are you ahead of or behind the beat?

Then at the Arnold Arboretum School, I chatted with another parent—how can we get the kids better at writing? Maybe some sort of competition/ contest would help? I think being able to write is more important than calculus, for example, although I'm not dissing math literacy.

Oma comes in the living room, looking for John's missing water bottle.

Yours, Phil

September 13, Wednesday, 7:09 AM

Dearest Al,

We're at the breakfast table, and John is singing: "Can I have something to eat—yogurt, jam and honey?" Oma stands up to get it for him, and Margo yawns.

I scratch my beard.

Now John is talking about the World Cup Qualifiers, and Oma is serving him cereal.

Yesterday she called me because she was sick, with a headache, vomiting, and weakness, but today she seems to have recovered.

I picked up a novel from the Little Free Library, "Replay," by Ken Grimwood. What would you do if you could live your life over again? And again? And again?

I could've made different choices at time branch points. But I'm happy about where I am.

Yours, Phil

September 15, Friday, 5:19 AM

Dearest Al,

I'm at the breakfast table trying a new experiment. I'm adding writing to my morning routine. Yesterday, for some reason I didn't do any journaling. I did run, go to Planet Fitness, take John to school with Oma and pick him up, do MEGA, go boxing, go to work, and even practice violin. But if writing is central to my Health and Healing, I must write. So my morning plan includes these components; weighing myself; meditation; coffee; kitchen weightlifting/pushups; journaling. And feeding Margo, of course.

Last night at Malcolm X, I saw a young patient who affected me. In his 20s, he is depressed and my prior attempts to cheer him up haven't worked. I even told him I'd been admitted to a psych ward, to destigmatize things and give him a little hope. We'll see if he can turn it around.

Health and Healing—improve your wellness—that's my motto. And I've started putting up signs around JP to advertise my website and email newsletter. I feel like my recovery is connected to the health of everyone in my neighborhood.

Yours, Phil

September 16, Saturday, 4:55 PM

Dearest Al,

John's friend Mack Mickelson is over for a playdate—they are engrossed in ping pong.

This morning I woke up sick. Since then I've been trying to relax and heal.

Oma is washing dishes.

The boys just went down in the basement on a house tour: I'm yawning.

What do I want to say...

Last night Jacob Kahn, Ilana Rosenberg, and family invited

us over for Rosh Hashanah/ Shabbat dinner—it was quite nice. Ilana asked me about what I think of the Arnold Arboretum School. How to balance wanting the best for John with desiring all Boston kids to succeed?

I have no answers—the black/white, rich/poor, public/private system is a quagmire. All I can say is we must keep striving for quality and equity. All kids deserve a top-notch education. More and better schools; less money spent on bombs.

Yours, Phil

September 17, Sunday, 5:33 AM

Dearest Al,

Last night we ate well—quesadillas; played table tennis; made love—life is good.

Today I'm going for my last long run before the Minneapolis marathon; John has swimming class, and his first soccer practice.

And there's the Physicians for a National Health Program (PNHP) backyard picnic—fighting for health justice.

Yesterday I finished reading Ken Grimwood's novel "Replay." It was problematic in some ways, but the central idea, that we could live our lives over and over, was compelling. It told the story of 43-year-old Jeff Winston, trapped in a tepid marriage and dead-end job, who dies of a heart attack, but then, Groundhog Day style, wakes up at age 18, in 1963 in his Emory University dorm room. And he lives his life again and again, in different ways.

I'm not Jeff Winston, but I was entertained, and I want to live my life, now.

Yours, Phil

September 18, Monday, 4:55 AM

Dearest Al,

I'm up early—I had some crazy dreams then woke up having to pee. In my dream I was camping with a group of people at an old-time music festival in the forest. Lots of fiddling/banjo, but things turned ugly for some reason. And someone—Oma, I believe, was taking the lug nuts off the cars so the wheels were getting loose and falling off.

What does that represent?

Yesterday my 20-mile-run around Castle Island was good. I passed the Harbor Point Fitness Center trying to "Replay" 2015-2018. But you weren't on the exercise bike, dad. John and I weren't in the swimming pool. We weren't going over to 307 for Blueberry Couscous Cake.

Then, we went to Grandma's—she was frazzled because her internet wasn't working, but we went for a nice walk by the tennis courts. Later, John enjoyed soccer at English High School. Oma told me of conflict between the two of them.

Sigh.

The PNHP picnic was good. I told the group of my interest in music therapy. I came home early and John and I played ping pong—he beat me for the first time!

Yours, Phil

September 19, Tuesday, 5:21 AM

Dearest Al,

Yesterday, I visited Grandma again—a mitzvah, perhaps. She was better; we drank tea and listened to Madame Butterfly, which you had loved. It rained.

I need a new violin bow—I knocked mine off the stand and the tip snapped. Good luck, I hope.

And last night, John played soccer for >1 hour through the deluge. The kids were soaked, but cackling. When we got home, Oma beat me in ping pong, but finally I defeated her—once.

Yours, Phil

September 20, Wednesday, 5:22 AM

Dearest Al,

A new legal pad, after my morning meditation. A cup of coffee, a banana, a piece of cranberry-walnut bread with peanut butter. I'll run at 6 AM with Ron and perhaps Lester. Life is good.

Every day we start anew, with hope, like the "Replay" novel I wrote about a couple days ago. Groundhog Day. I told Dr. Fanon about "Replay"—certainly not to recommend the novel for its literary value, just for the concept of memory and reliving our lives.

Our dreams from past years, our work and aspirations; the people we have loved (yesterday I spontaneously brought Laura's name up to Dr. Fanon); the people we love now (Kathy's alarm clock, coincidentally or not, is going off)...

Yesterday I was thinking about Rudolph Virchow. I'm not running for Massachusetts State Representative, but why couldn't it I?

Virchow, the German physician and founder of social medicine, was a member of the Reichstag from 1880-1893. It's just an idea.

Today is for MEGA:)

Yours, Phil

September 21, Thursday, 5:31 AM

Dearest Al,

Yesterday I was daydreaming and writing about running for

political office. Today, I just want to get our microwave fixed.

It's been broken for a long time, more than a year. In July of last year I was in touch with an electrician because I wasn't sure if the problem was the microwave itself, or the circuit breaker. She told me to get an extension cord and try it on a different circuit.

Now, Kathy brought it up twice, because she wants more countertop space—the second microwave she purchased could find a new home if we could get the finicky built-in one repaired or replaced.

So now I have an extension cord out of the closet, and I'm planning where I will plug it in. But either way, we will need a new microwave, or some sort of repair done to our circuit breaker?

The bigger issue is how can I get better at marking things off my to-do list, "crossing the finish line" so to speak. It's the same with this DDD book, my CD, and the unionization...

Yours, Phil

September 22, Friday, 5:20 AM

Dearest Al,

More on "crossing the finish line" and checking things off my to-do list. It can be hard to do when you are in uncharted waters.

With the microwave, I tested it yesterday, and I'm pretty certain the problem is the Frigidaire unit itself. I know an appliance store here in JP, so I have a plan.

But something like my DDD book—it's daunting, like running my first marathon was. At least with that 26.2 mile race, I had guidance from Ron and others. With this book, I feel like I'm trying to navigate the Pacific Ocean alone, on a papyrus raft.

It's probably how my patient "J" feels. I saw him last night—a man with HIV and depression, eight psych ward stays—my doppelgänger (I only had one psych ward stay, and it was brief—because of my race, English skills, education, monetary resources, family, etc).

Malcolm X wasn't terrible last night. On the one hand, not so many patients showed up. But on the other hand I was drowning in MEGA.

Yours, Phil

5

Autumn

September 23, Saturday, 5:28 AM

Dearest Al,

Shabbat. I'll rest for 12 hours, because I'm a half-Jew.

Yesterday, I left off thinking about a health worker walkout; my Satyagraha daydream recurs. I don't know. To organize a (nonviolent) revolt you have to bring people together.

Today is a day of relaxation, of spiritual calm. My phone is locked up; the timer won't the KSafe open until 6:50 PM. I'll use willpower to stay off the computers.

I was actually thinking of going to Spanish Mass at St. Thomas Aquinas at 4 PM. It's around the corner from our house on South Street. Not because I want to convert to Catholicism, but to remember my childhood—Nanna and Grandpa in Toledo; Midnight Mass at Rosary Cathedral. I guess I'm also a half-Catholic, although I don't identify as such. The scandals are too much for me.

But here I am, in this labyrinth called life. My friends, family, neighbors, and patients are in a similar spiral.

Yours, Phil

September 24, Sunday 6:23 AM

Dearest Al,

Yesterday it was a rainy day in the labyrinth. I started out in Korean school, in the intermediate/ advanced class. I was lost, but it inspired me to study Korean for a minute each day. Tiny habits (BJ Fogg, Stanford).

I didn't go to Mass; instead we went to Grandma's. We listened to Phil Ochs, "There But for Fortune."

Today, I want to repeat the Health and Healing worksheet I filled out with Oma. Hopefully it will point us in the direction of our goals—on our holiday card last year, I announced to my friends I would have my book in their mailbox — and that's only 99 days away. Unless a miracle occurs, and an agent/publisher appear out of nowhere, I need to type up / print this book.

Yours, Phil

September 25, Monday, 5:11 AM

Dearest Al,

We did the worksheet yesterday (Oma's only)—her answers were roughly the same as 2 weeks ago, except that she has a new tiny habit—first thing in the morning, out loud, she says to herself, "I'm going to have a great day!" Positive psychology.

My book—98 days remaining. Write, read, edit, transcribe, distribute it to 100 friends before the new year.

Today is Yom Kippur—the Day of Atonement. A day of repentance, to God, to others. Maybe I'll pass by Nehar Shalom synagogue.

Rabbi Michael Lerner ("the peace rabbi," according to Aunt Mary Ann), is having online services, but I didn't sign up. I'll do my own Atonement.

Yours, Phil

September 26, Tuesday, 5:18 AM

Dearest Al,

Here we are. I'm eating an egg sandwich, looking at a letter you wrote to me on 10/28/2010, my 30th birthday. I was still in San Diego, in the middle of my internal medicine residency. You were living in Kentucky. I reread the letter, one of a few handwritten pieces of correspondence to have survived, written by you to me.

In it, you wish that *each of my tomorrows exceed each of my todays.*"

And I suppose they are.

I seem to be maintaining my health, becoming more Zen even as I face new challenges—Grandma's frailty, Kathy's moods.

I just try to do my habits, keep checking my checkboxes.

Speaking of Marathons, Minneapolis is only 5 days away. Keep the marathon mindset. Write John a letter today, and Oma a birthday card.

Yours, Phil

September 27, Wednesday, 5:24 AM

Dearest Al,

Imagining a better future. I stumbled upon a book which discusses the promise of positive imagery in improving our lives. That's a theme for today, along with the "thought record." These are used in Cognitive Behavioral Therapy, and I wrote up my own after a talk with Dr. Fanon yesterday. If my emotions get too up or down, I'll whip out my "mindful check-in" sheet and write how I'm feeling. I'd also like to translate it into Spanish and Cape Verdean Creole for my patients.

Yours, Phil

September 28, Thursday, 5:21 AM

Dearest Al,

Yesterday's clinic finished up with another patient requesting a N-648 form—inability to learn English and civics, for immigration purposes. Her reasons—major depression, diabetes, chronic pain, low education level, low literacy. She is in her 70s, from the Dominican Republic—and yet, reminded me of my mother.

Immigration and asylum in the United States—what a broken system. And in Boston, we are 1000+ miles from the border, where things seem to have gotten worse in recent months. It makes me remember my years in San Diego/Tijuana.

Yours, Phil

September 29, Friday 5:25 AM

Dearest Al,

Don't sweat the small stuff—that's all I have to say. My patient last night told me why she moved from Dorchester to the suburbs a decade ago—her son had been shot.

Yours, Phil

September 29, Friday 6:29 PM

Dearest Al,

I'm at 30,000 feet—JetBlue. Someone is speaking Spanish behind me. We're over Lake Michigan. I think Sleeping Bear Dunes is down below—memories of my childhood.

So I have a 2-day retreat in Minnesota—to unwind with friends, relax, and run a marathon.

I miss John, Oma, Margo, and Grandma, but so far so good.

Clinic this morning was ok but also difficult because we had a "Code Blue." However it turned out to be a false alarm—a woman had vagaled in the phlebotomy room during a blood draw.

Still, to be interrupted by that overhead page, "Code Blue," from the conversation I was having with my patient, a man whose son is suffering from mental illness, was disruptive at best and a little traumatic. "Code Blue."

In the airport, things were crowded and stressful. Now, far above the clouds, in a mixture of blues and whites, it's reasonably peaceful.

Yours, Phil

September 30, Saturday, 6:26 AM, Central time

Dearest Al,

One of Yadid's kids is playing the piano. I heard snippets of Lightly Row along with other random notes. Now I hear voices. Saturday morning in Minneapolis!

Yours, Phil

October 1, Sunday, 6:15 PM, Central time

Dearest Al,

I'm in the Minneapolis airport, listening to Jordu—Clifford Brown—and having the time of my life, despite the JetBlue delay; marathon cancellation this morning 2 hours before the race (heat stroke danger). In life, you must improvise. We still ran ten miles.

Yours, Phil

October 2, Monday, 5 AM, Central time

Dearest Al,

I just had a nice, hot shower at Yadid's. Yes, I'm still in Minneapolis. Not only was my marathon cancelled, the JetBlue flight was delayed until 9 AM—mechanical issues. So I took a $40+ taxi back to Yadid's house, where they graciously put me up (again!). And now I'm going to brush my teeth then find my way back to the airport. It's a slog, and I'm sleep deprived, but I'll get home, somehow...

"This Little Light of Mine... I'm gonna let it shine..." and "Guantanamera..." and other songs will give me hope as I try to journey home.

Yours, Phil

October 3, Tuesday, 4:50 AM, Eastern standard time (!)
Dearest Al,
My body is readjusting to Boston, so I'm up a little early drinking coffee. I'm ok. I survived the 26 hour Minneapolis JetBlue saga/crisis with my mental health intact (I think). Don't Worry, Be Happy. When confronted with the fear of death (during takeoff), pray: Baruch Atao Adonai...

Last night back in Jamaica Plain—dining room basketball with John—he was doing his spin moves, dunks. Gratitude.

I loved seeing Yadid, Farley, and Harry in Minnesota, but it's super nice to be home.

This morning I'm daydreaming about Farley's backyard "Redwood Outdoor Sauna"—it looks like an enormous wooden barrel with a glass door. They haven't used it yet, because they still need to get the stones, but it's going to be great. And it's wood fired—I'd love one!

But how to convince Oma (and our upstairs neighbors)? And is it worth $5000+ to have a hot sauna on snowy winter nights? Probably!

Anyway, I'm at home.

Good fiddle tunes in Minnesota, playing on Harry/Clyde

Davenport's old violin!
Yours, Phil

October 4, Wednesday, 5:36 AM
Dearest Al,
It's your Yahrzeit. Three years ago today, you died, in Kentucky. I'm sitting next to the electronic candle which will "burn" for 24 hours in remembrance.

I have distinct memories from when I was growing up, of Yahrzeits for Red and Marjorie, your parents. An office lamp would be left on for a night and day, in the Jewish tradition. The Yahrzeit seemed to be the thing you held most sacred, along with caring about cemeteries, ancestry, and geneology....the stories and gravestones of the past.

So I won't think about the small bumps in the road yesterday, the conflicts. Rather, I will remember my father, the wonderful man who told me to "always be nice to Kathy." The man who cared most about John's (and my) education.

That's why, last night, I joined the School Site Council as a representative. To be more involved with John's school. More knowledgeable. To have a little bit of a voice, at the Arb. I still believe it's a nice, wholesome school—and how can we help it grow?

More social events; a Little Free Library?
Yours, Phil

October 5, Thursday, 5:26 AM
Dearest Al,
Today I want to talk about money. Sure, I'm a doctor, and we have some cash saved—BUT. I'm part-time, in primary care, at a federally qualified community health center in a poor

neighborhood (almost all of my patients are living in poverty, on medicaid).

I have a lot more expenses than I'd like—for example, legal fees. Today I have to go to Van's office in downtown Boston and be present in front of the state medical board. I'll probably get a bill for >$1000 for his preparation, time spent emailing, doing the Zoom, etc. I think I've paid well over ten thousand dollars to Van and Hannah.

And then there's saving for college and retirement. I think we have a decent financial plan, but I'm not really sure—it depends on the stock market.

Financially I am presumably much better off than most of my Malcolm X health care worker colleagues. And, my last patient yesterday was a 70-year-old man from the Dominican Republic who works concessions at Fenway Park. I'm certain he is in a precarious financial situation.

But even if we unionize, will Malcolm X health care workers and patients continue to languish?

Yours, Phil

October 6, Friday, 5:25 AM

Dearest Al,

I went before the medical board yesterday. Nothing terrible happened, but I doubt I'll ever get off this probation agreement. And I owe $1400 to Van.

I love my lawyer :)

Later, I saw patients at Malcolm X—an older man with hand arthritis but otherwise well; a woman from Cape Verde with whom I got to practice my Portuguese; a lady with chronic back pain who still knew how to laugh; a man with asthma; another with a stomachache. The patients keep on coming. It's

overwhelming.
Yours, Phil

October 7, Saturday, 6:07 AM
Dearest Al,
One thing about taking care of a large number of Cape Verdean patients is I learn about their culture, food, and music. For example, most of them eat cachupa, a casserole made from corn and meat or seafood. The traditional music of Cabo Verde is called Morna. There once was a singer from the island of Sao Vicente named Cesaria Evora. She died a few years ago, but was famous for her ballads. One in particular, "Saudade," speaks of the sadness of the Cape Verdean people dealing with loss.

I actually tried to learn to sing that song, working on the guitar chords and Portuguese pronunciation with a Mozambican friend of mine, several years ago. He had moved to Massachusetts to attend Berklee and stayed to become a professional musician. I wonder what became of him? We lost touch during the pandemic...
Yours, Phil

October 8, Sunday, 5:47 AM
Dearest Al,
Autumn. The taste of apple cider.
We had a scary moment yesterday—John was playing baseball and he was accidentally kicked in the head by one of his friends fathers' who was trying to make a tag (they both slipped).
"There But for Fortune," the Phil Ochs song.
Korean class was good. And we met our teacher's husband—turns out he is in a wheelchair. I found that surprising, his disability. It was like we were in a Pedro Almodovar movie.

John had a playdate in the afternoon, so Kathy and I got some alone time which was good, if you get my drift :)

I stopped by a brunch with my COVID Zoom meditation group. It was nice to see them in person.

I made some edits to this manuscript, changing names to pseudonyms and fictionalizing things so real, living people wouldn't get too offended. Today — running, soccer, fiddle, a visit to Grandma.

Yours, Phil

October 9, Monday, 5:34 AM

Dearest Al,

Indigenous People's Day (AKA Columbus Day). Four decades ago I was born, in "*Columbus*," Ohio. I'm thinking how Christopher Columbus treated the indigenous people he found, kind of like how the Israeli military (and Hamas) are treating the people in that Apartheid state. This war is horrific, especially because America is complicit, with our military-industrial complex and support of human rights violations. Where is the peace movement? We blindly accept these wars...

Next to me is a book—"Don't Sweat the Small Stuff... and it's all small stuff — simple ways to keep the little things from taking over your life." True... focus on my mental health, my family, my neighborhood... and yet to be a person of conscience who pays taxes which go to the Pentagon, how do I stay silent, when Netanyahu is about to flatten Gaza; when Ukraine-Russia is a powder keg; when North and South Korea are on a precipice.

I'm not "sweating the small stuff," I'm writing about the big stuff—a plea for peace and reconciliation. Stop the shooting; the dehumanization of people different from us.

Yours, Phil

October 10, Tuesday, 5:33 AM
Dearest Al,
The Eye of the Tiger.
Yesterday, after the North Korea health zoom, and dropping John off at baseball clinic, and the Indigenous People's Day festival in Newton, I had a violin lesson on Bob's back porch. Our last session had focused on the song Jordu, but today I asked to study the classic 1980s hit by Survivor, "Eye of the Tiger."

We worked on chopping, strum bowing, a la Tracy Silverman, and singing. It turns out the tessatura, the vocal range of "Eye of the Tiger," is only one octave. But because I can't hit the high C (falsetto), we had to transpose the tune down from C minor to A minor. I hope John will learn it with me.

What else? I continue to be highly disturbed by the war in Gaza and Israel. I wrote a petition on change.org calling for a ceasefire and deescalation—but I didn't email it out to my list. I'm not sure why not, when Palestinians (and Israelis) are about to be slaughtered.

Yours, Phil

October 11, Wednesday, 5:17 AM
Dearest Al,
Last night at the Arnold Arboretum School, there a bit of controversy. You see, the principal had been saying a Land Acknowledgement to the Wampanoag Native Americans, which states that white settlers had invaded and colonized the region. Several parents didn't like the use of the word "white..." This made me think of Israel and Gaza—Palestinians say the land was Arab first; Israelis claim it was theirs.

Land, power, history, tribalism... boy is this stuff complex, and it often leads to genocide. The petition I wrote for a ceasefire, and peace in the Middle East, has only 1 signature—mine.

Back to the Arnold Arboretum School—our focus should be helping children succeed, a better quality education, more resilient kids... having fun.

Yours, Phil

October 12, Thursday, 5:30 AM

Dearest Al,

I keep trying. Yesterday I saw a patient in his 20s, a man from Boston who was in primary care clinic for a sore throat. After we came up with a plan regarding antibiotics, I spent the rest of our visit focused on weight loss strategies because he weighed 295 lbs. I advised him to make small changes in terms of habits—to weigh himself every morning and do exercise before going to work, as I do. I hope he might undergo a health transformation, before the inevitable type 2 diabetes, high cholesterol, and hypertension set in.

As for me, I'm 183 lbs, in a new steady state down from 190 lbs two months ago. I want to lose three more pounds before the new year, which is only twelve weeks away.

Yours, Phil

October 13, Friday, 5:17 AM

Dearest Al,

Friday the thirteenth. I'm eating an egg with toast.

Last night I saw a patient who really needs help—a young woman on Suboxone for opiate use disorder, active hepatitis C needing treatment, knee pain from prior MRSA osteomyelitis, and depression/ PTSD.

She was doing ok, in that she's in recovery, and not using fentanyl/ heroin anymore, but she is at risk for relapse and needs behavioral health therapy, job training, etc. But having money is a trigger for her to use opiates, she tells me, so she almost doesn't *want* to get a job.

Complex stuff, and she needs assistance. It frustrated me, as always — our broken health system, and a lack of resources for addiction, mental health, trauma. She could easily relapse and overdose; or she could pull through this tenuous phase. This patient encounter made me text Monica Potts and the other activists... I don't want to leave medicine—I'm a good doctor and I enjoy it. But this job is unsustainable, impossible, and we need a white coat walkout.

Yours, Phil

October 14, Saturday, 5:43 AM

Dearest Al,

Well, here I am, reflecting on yesterday's clinic—the last patient I saw, a young woman, was apparently the victim of domestic violence. She declined when I suggested she see our advocate, or our behavioral health therapist, or consider going to the police for a restraining order. She seemed overwhelmed and deadened—and left. All I can do now is pray for her and her child, that they find their way to a safer environment...

And Gaza/Israel? The same prayer—that the Israeli military cease fire, and deescalate...

And yet, we must keep living life. Last night we went to the Danceathon fundraiser at the Arnold Arboretum School... John had fun.

Yours, Phil

October 15, Sunday, 6:18 AM

Dearest Al,

Sure, yesterday had some tough moments, like when John and Kathy (and I) were struggling with distressing emotions—anger, sadness, etc. It seemed to start when our son (almost) refused to go to Korean School, and that was very triggering for Oma...

But eventually we deescalated the conflicts, and I think we have greater empathy for when others are suffering. I wrote out some "mindful check-ins," from our different perspectives (fictionalized)—can we imagine what someone else is experiencing, and write it out? We must learn to take others' perspectives, to build peace in our homes...

And Korean School yesterday turned out to be good. I feel like I'm making some progress (baby steps).

I also took John to baseball. And I ran 14 miles. So—onward, we keep the "marathon mindset" and we push through our adversity... "Keep going..." and "it takes a team..." said Diana Nyad, who swam from Havana to Key West...

Yours, Phil

October 16, Monday, 5:20 AM
Dearest Al,

My "family team" is finally clicking... Saturday we had a lot of rough spots, but yesterday we got in an improved rhythm. It wasn't perfect, but we did a better job listening to each other and Kathy and John kept their emotions in check. We had a swimming lesson, a play date with Mack Mickelson, a soccer game over at English High School, the block party for Calle Santa Rosa, and we visited Grandma. What loose ends did I pick up on?

Balazs Varga has some sort of knee injury—maybe tendonitis. I wonder if we can help him out with that?

Thomas Lloyd played the tenor guitar at the block party as I fiddled. That was nice—the first time we made music together.

Grandma was a little better, and I was grateful to Kathy for fixing her computer and talking to her.

So here we are. It's another week. I am, as always, far behind on MEGA, and Malcolm X paperwork, and I need to carve out some real time for that.

The clinical skills assessment contract for Doctor Evaluation, Inc is finally executed, so I predict they are going to show up at Malcolm X sometime this week. They'll observe me seeing patients for 8 hours in the clinic, review my notes in MEGA, and my CME, and then make their report to the medical board and Physician Help Inc.

I can't say I am expecting Doctor Evaluation, Inc, to write a nice assessment after what happened with the neuropsychological testing last year with Dr. Runtsky. I think it's a real possibility I will lose my medical license.

But maybe I'm wrong—I'll stay positive. Stay positive.

I learned that on Blake 11, the inpatient psych ward, at Man's Greatest Hospital back in 2020.

Yours, Phil

October 17, Tuesday, 5:14 AM

Dearest Al,

Here I am, with my bagel and banana, my almond butter, as the coffee brews in the Cuisinart, and I think about yesterday's fitness session with Manny Alvarez. He is an exercise scientist, a certified strength and conditioning specialist and a certified sports nutritionist, with a PhD. I saw one of his ads for a free evaluation at the swimming pool and sent him a text. For about 25 minutes he had me do squats, pushups, sit-ups, and hold a plank. I decided not to sign up because of cost, but the session did make me realize the importance of accountability. I've lost almost 10 pounds (I weighed in at 181 this morning), but if I want to continue to improve I need to make time for proper weight-lifting sessions at Planet Fitness.

I don't want to turn into a male model (Manny also seems to do that in his spare time), but I wouldn't mind getting in better shape. It's something I can *potentially* control in this wacky world.

What else?

During my violin lesson yesterday with Bob Parker, we focused on the K-Pop song "For Lovers Who Hesitate ( ), by Jannabi. Bob wants me to take it apart and then create a chord chart. I'm also trying to learn the lyrics for my Saturday morning Korean class.

Life is busy.

And, as you know, I'm deeply troubled by what's going on in Gaza and Israel, because of my half-Jewish heritage, but also because I am a human being who cares about human rights. Why are Palestinian children being bombed? Why have I been virtually silent on this situation even though it's been going on for over a week?

I think of organizing a vigil in Jamaica Plan with Danny and Ellie, my neighbors. What's the potential downside? That there might be a pro-Israel neighbor who is offended? That a neo-Nazi group finds out about us and decides to take a potshot? That's possible, of course, in America.

But the ethical imperative to bear witness to human suffering, to call out for peace, seems essential. I can ask Kathy if she approves of a vigil.

Today we have a signing of an irrevocable trust at our estate

planning attorney's office in Wellesley. Money is complicated.
Yours, Phil

October 18, Wednesday, 5:12 AM
Dearest Al,
I'm worried about Monica Potts. She's said she's thinking of resigning from Malcolm X, even if we *do* win the union election. She doesn't get along with Dr. Duva—not that I appreciate our new boss's approach, either...

And she is sending intense emails and texts about the Palestinians... I guess I am doing the same, but I don't know... we have to keep our equanimity and control what we can—our health, even as Gaza burns.

But back to Dr. Duva—she is doing two jobs — Dr. Trump's and Dr. Roach's. She must be under a lot of stress even if she doesn't show it. Of course, the low-wage Malcolm X health workers, like custodians, call center, medical assistants, PCAs, home health workers, etc, are under much more pressure than our chief medical officer, because they can barely pay their rent.

On the union Zoom last night Freddy said we just have to wait for the National Labor Relations Board, but we must keep organizing, and trying to get more members and build power.

Meanwhile, I've been texting with Pluto, because an opportunity has come up to apply for an executive MBA program for physicians at Brandeis University. He and I always complain about being doctors, and maybe doing this would give us some flexibility to pursue different directions (?). The program starts in January 2024.

But I remember what you said back in 2020 when I was trying to take on new activities—focus on your job, your current responsibilities. That means (gasp) cleaning up my MEGA

InBasket, seeing patients today, and finishing my DDD, this book.

Yours, Phil

October 19, Thursday, 6:47 AM

Dearest Al,

I'm back from a run with Joey, hill repeats and then a lap of Jamaica Pond. And here I am, thinking about *character*. Isn't that the most important thing, to treat others with respect? Are we doing a good job with John in teaching him our values? Is he kind to others?

I can't control what he learns from his classmates, teachers, and from society, but I can demonstrate empathy, day-by-day.

Yours, Phil

October 20, Friday, 5:11 AM

Dearest Al,

Babe Cohen is here—my best friend from high school flew in from Washington DC last night. I just served him coffee in bed. Supposedly he'll get up and join us on this morning's run, but we will see... I remember when we first met—8th grade, during a Lexington Youth Soccer Association game—he was on the opposing team. He was short, had long hair, and was a striker—the game was at Masterson Station Park. And here we are, 28 years later... unbelievable.

Babe was a freelance science writer for years, but recently made a career change and now works for the federal government.

He emerges from the bedroom—"I see you have emotion cards," he says, pointing to our wall.

Yours, Phil

October 21, Saturday 6:04 AM

Dearest Al,

Continuing on the theme of "Emotion Cards," we do have orange cards hanging from a string on our kitchen wall, with drawn/colored faces—"Neutral, Excited, Loving, Happy, Angry, Shy, etc."

And this is important, I think—understanding our own emotions, where we are at this moment, what day-to-day activities we can do to raise our spirits...

Speaking of that, I enjoyed beating Babe in ping pong.

Yours, Phil

October 22, Sunday, 5:07 AM

Dearest Al,

Yesterday was good. I ran 13 miles with Ron and company—he encouraged me to consider the Brandeis executive MBA program for physicians. A business degree would be good for me, he said. For someone like me, who is to the left of Bernie Sanders :)

Then I had Korean school, and later on Babe Cohen and I hung out again. Ping pong, fiddle — old time, klezmer.

Yours, Phil

October 23, Monday, 5:28 AM

Dearest Al,

Why was I silent during the Iraq war, and Afghanistan war as well? Will I remain silent as people die in Gaza/Israel?

I was texting with Emilio, a college friend, yesterday. He describes himself as techno-optimistic.

I am as impressed as anyone with refrigerators, laptops, iPhones... and I enjoy these technologies. But I am a human optimist, or a humanist.

People need to come together to protest injustice, to fight for peace. Technology—bombs, drones, nukes—could kill all of us. Building the beloved community.

Yours, Phil

October 24, Tuesday, 5:26 AM

Dearest Al,

Kathy was struggling last night—she's got the "blues" and can't seem to come up with a plan to reduce her irritability. I don't think my ideas and suggestions helped her.

It's not ok—but the best I can come up with is staying even-keeled myself, living my life—and trying to get couples counseling restarted. It fell off over the summer when Dr. Park finished his fellowship at Man's Greatest.

What else? MEGA—ugh. My book, my DDD—time is short—I need to make sure Zeke got the manuscript.

Yours, Phil

October 25, Wednesday, 5:17 AM

Dearest Al,

So it goes.

I was busy with MEGA yesterday and I didn't call the couple's therapist back. I did get Kathy some flowers, and a pizza for the family. But then I fell asleep early, around 8:45 PM.

I had the vague sensation that something wasn't right, and I woke up at 12:30 AM and "caught" (discovered) Kathy still awake, watching videos on her iPhone in the Orange Room.

"So it goes," to quote Kurt Vonnegut.

(I know his son, Dr. Mark Vonnegut—a Boston pediatrician and author who is also living with bipolar. He's a funny writer, just like his father).

Yours, Phil

October 26, Thursday, 5:18 AM

Dearest Al,

Onward! Life is busy, but we keep going. Last night, at our kids' soccer practice, Thomas Lloyd offered to read my book! I'm going to surprise him and take him up on his offer. Tom is a nice guy, a scientist, originally from Alaska, who plays the tenor banjo among other instruments. He came to our block party, as you may recall.

He has a goofy, whimsical smile and is fun to chat with. We particularly enjoy talking about music. (Gaza/Israel, and North Korea, maybe not so much). No matter.

Thanks, Thomas!

Yours, Phil

October 27, Friday, 4:50 AM

Dearest Al,

I'm up a little early—not sure why—probably stress from work, Gaza, etc. But it's ok—I don't think I am getting manic. Tonight I will sleep better.

Yesterday a couple friends from my San Diego days, Noah and Sophia stopped by, with their kids—they are visiting New England for a family event. We had a delightful chat and stroll through the Arnold Arboretum; the leaves were at their peak and it was sunny. It was nice to see old friends from residency, and their kids.

Our lives have diverged—one is a psychiatrist, the other a hospitalist, and their children have some health concerns, but they are doing well. "There But For Fortune."

Malcolm X last night was chaotic. The first patient arrived on time but the front desk didn't register her, so she got upstairs to primary care 42 minutes late. It made the entire evening backed up and difficult—I was running behind with all my patients, and off balance. But I'm not giving up. I have my goals.

Yours, Phil

October 28, Saturday, 5:19 AM

Dearest Al,

My 43rd birthday—Kathy wrote me a very nice card. I'm happy.

More tomorrow—I'm going to go running. Hopefully I'll get up to around 17-18 miles before Korean class.

Yours, Phil

October 29, Sunday, 7:00 AM

Dearest Al,

Yesterday's birthday highlight—John doing the dance to Michael Jackson's "Thriller" in the lobby of Grandma's apartment building.

Yours, Phil

October 30, Monday, 5:22 AM

Dearest Al,

It was a good weekend. Yesterday we had a potluck in the community garden next to our house. One of the gardeners baked hot pizzas in a metal oven placed on the picnic table. Despite the light rain, it was fun—I chatted with a video game designer from North Carolina and it brought back memories of the old days in Kentucky.

John's soccer game was lopsided and soggy, but enjoyable. On the sidelines, I talked with a local architect—the majority of his work is with computers, CAD, etc. As much as I dislike STEM, I wonder if Joe's math and technology education is strong enough?

Later on, he had a playdate at the home of one of his friends from the Arnold Arboretum School—football, etc. And as he often does at the end of a playdate, he refused to go home :(

I found myself getting frustrated as almost 45 minutes passed in their living room, the kids running in circles, giggling.

Yours, Phil

October 31, Tuesday, 5:20 AM

Dearest Al,

More drama at the Arnold Arboretum School. One of John's classmates tried to trip him yesterday—the same kid who spat at him previously, and is generally disruptive. Troubling—plus nothing from the teacher or principal about these incidents. I could forgive that, except for prior events at the Arb, along with neighboring schools. Sadly, it seems like BPS has a culture of bullying which often gets glossed over or covered up.

But what can I do? Would suburban public schools or private schools really be that much better? They would have their own set of problems.

Organize.

It's in my DNA.

I'll try to talk to Balazs and Sally Varga, Jacob Kahn, and other parents.

I'm also on the school site council, so that's a position of privilege.

Yours, Phil

November 1, Wednesday, 5:26 AM

Dearest Al,

"How much do I love you? I'll tell you no lie..." I have the jazz standard "How Deep is the Ocean" stuck in my head.

As the stress at Malcolm X mounts—the latest is I learned I have Physician Help Inc forms that are a month late; the Doctor Evaluation Inc skills assessment needs to be set up; and I have MEGA overload.

So I retreat to Frank Sinatra.

Thanks, Bob—my violin teacher has me trying to learn this tune in all 12 keys.

What else?

Yesterday Dr. Fanon said to me ($125)—"schedule MEGA" on my calendar.

Basic time management skills, which I am still learning at age 43 (!)

Then last night, Margo and I took John and his Arb School friend trick or treating on Dunster Road in Jamaica Plain. It was a big party—dancing ghosts, a live band, etc—good times.

Margo ate it up.

Yours, Phil

November 2, Thursday, 5:13 AM

Dearest Al,

Where do I want to be in 5 years? I'll be 48; Kathy will be 56; John will be 13; Margo will be 8. My mom will be 78 (of course this assumes we are all still alive). I'd like to be running marathons, playing violin, writing/doing advocacy, and practicing medicine part-time, if possible. Despite everything.

Yesterday, a patient informed me he owns a '357 and a '38 at home—he didn't threaten me, but that revelation of gun ownership was frightening.

So yes, despite encounters like that one, I still enjoy seeing patients.

It's just that MEGA is harmful to my mental health, so from an occupational health perspective, I need to limit my exposure to our electronic medical record, and our health system.

It's as if I were a coal miner who enjoyed being underground but wanted to avoid getting sick with black lung.

Yours, Phil

November 3, Friday, 5:35 AM

Dearest Al,

I'm tired.

That's all I'm going to say for today.

Yours, Phil

November 4, Saturday, 6:32 AM

Dearest Al,

Saturday morning, thank God. Even though I didn't see that many patients this week, it was a long one. At multiple points in time I felt my stress levels rising—a frog on the stove in a pan of water, slowly boiling.

The issue is I don't live in a bubble, and I am an empathetic person. I think of the novel, "The Parable of the Sower" by Octavia Butler. The protagonist is Lauren Olamina, who deeply feels the pain of others.

Margo starts barking wildly next to the back door. I pick her up and carry her to the orange room, to the cushioned chair, and set her down. She sits, eventually sleeps.

Yes, perhaps because of my bipolar I feel the distress of other people quite deeply. My patients—for example the illiterate, isolated man who was fired from Malcolm X this week because of disruptive behavior and pushing a health care worker. Clinic security caught it on video—and I was tasked with doing a telemedicine visit with him to check in.

He sounded so lost.

And Kathy—after a week of working in primary care, all she could do was sink into an audio book, "Angela's Ashes," and climb into bed.

But John wanted to build a model zeppelin airship—so the family did end up hanging out—even Margo.

Today I'm going to run 10 miles, then go to Korean class, then we have baseball, then we'll visit my mom. Tomorrow is John's birthday party.

Yours, Phil

November 5, Sunday, 5:25 AM, Daylight Savings Time

Dearest Al,

First world problems.

Margo barking early in the morning, awakening us.

John whining about wanting a play date, Kathy getting upset, emotional turmoil in our household.

Etc.

No bombs are dropping on us. We have plenty of food to eat, hobbies.

I got an email last night from our UCSD friends who are missionaries in the Democratic Republic of Congo, where civil war is an omnipresent threat.

But our first world problems—MEGA, the Boston Public Schools, Doctor Evaluation, Inc, our emotional roller coaster—are real issues for Kathy, John, and myself.

And Lewiston, Maine reminds us of the insane number of guns in America, and the fact that this country could erupt into a real civil war at any time.

Hyperbole?

War in Gaza, war in Ukraine, war in the Democratic Republic of Congo... we are not immune, here in the United States of America.

We need peace activists, and we need them now.

Yours, Phil

November 6, Monday, 4:54 AM

Dearest Al,

I'm up a bit early—Daylight Savings Time—my hypothalamus knows when it wants me to awaken.

Yesterday we had a nice day—John's swim lesson, soccer game, and birthday party. The kids ran around, played baseball, and bounced balloons in the air. The parents ate cheese, drank apple cider, chatted, and listened to Duke Ellington and John Coltrane as the sun set.

Fidel's dad updated me about Argentinian and Uruguayan rock music—I need to check his Whatsapp messages.

So here we are—another week. The theme of this week is loving kindness. When I see negativity in the world, or experience internal negative emotions, I will respond with love.

For example yesterday's soccer game was good, but it was almost spoiled by a couple of parents who were bossing the kids around, Bobby Knight style (RIP coach—and go Wildcats, boo Hoosiers).

Next time at soccer, I can respond internally with loving kindness.

Every morning, at the end of my meditation, I take one more deep breath and pray for loving kindness. I pray for health and healing for all.

Yours, Phil

November 7, Tuesday, 5:14 AM
Dearest Al,
Well here we are. John's ninth birthday is tomorrow. And I've been writing this DDD diary for almost a year. Dr. Phil's adventures in Boston, Los Angeles, Tijuana, Cape Cod, Vermont, South Korea, and Minneapolis. I'll write for three more weeks and then call it a day and self-publish this book. And what, dear reader, have you learned?

That I love MEGA? Not really :)

It's been a year of adventure/turmoil at Malcolm X Health Center, with Dr. Humble quitting, Dr. Trump getting fired, Dr. Roach quitting, Doctor Evaluation, Inc. And today I have another meeting with Physician Help Inc.

Groundhog Day.

The skills assessment still hasn't been scheduled, to my knowledge.

I also have psychoanalysis with Dr. Fanon, and a meeting with Dr. Daneeka.

And the National Labor Relations Board will mail the union election secret ballots next Monday.

I phoned Man's Greatest Hospital yesterday, to their couples counselor, and left a message. Kathy and I have been without a couples therapist since Dr. Park graduated from his fellowship in the summer.

In a few minutes I'll go running with Ron, Pablo, and Joey. The Manchester, New Hampshire marathon is on Sunday morning. I plan to drive up early, run the race, and then come home in the afternoon—a day trip.

Yours, Phil

November 8, Wednesday, 5:11 AM

Dearest Al,

It's John's ninth birthday today, and that makes up for my tossing and turning last night, my worries about Malcolm X and Doctor Evaluation, Inc.

I try to recall his birth, in 2014, at Tufts Medical Center, then the yearly November celebrations—in Chinatown, at Harbor Point, and in Jamaica Plain. It has been a privilege and a delight to be his father.

Happy birthday, son.

Yours, Phil

November 9, Thursday, 5:11 AM

Dearest Al,

I skipped my morning run; Pluto and Monica were texting me around 11:30 PM, and since I'm on call this week, I had my iPhone in the bedroom and I woke up with their messages. It's ok—I'm tapering for Sunday's marathon. Sleeping in is good.

John emerges from his bedroom, talking about Harry Potter. Kathy makes kimpop—eggs and brown rice rolled into seaweed. I eat my bagel with feta cheese and hot sauce—a weird breakfast. John yawns.

"Which of these is not my lunch," he asks, nibbling on some egg.

—

Recently I saw a patient, a middle-aged woman with schizoaffective disorder/bipolar type, and I really was thinking "there but for fortune." She is unemployed, obese, and still lives with her mother.

She seemed to be doing ok, stable on several antipsychotic medications, but told me her "mind is somewhere else" when she tries to watch TV or Youtube, or listen to gospel sermons.

She isn't anxious and doesn't hear voices; she just has difficulty focusing.

The lady almost reminds me of myself. Yesterday, during my psychoanalysis session with Dr. Fanon, we talked about how I struggle to focus on MEGA. I have difficulty putting MEGA on my calendar and getting my notes and messages done.

My "mind is somewhere else."

Yours, Phil

November 10, Friday, 6:21 AM

Dearest Al,

Today my mind is "here"—I had a good meditation a few minutes ago. Zen.

Yesterday was fine, with a bid of sad mixed in. The good: boxing; and music/art therapy. Even clinic was enjoyable—I saw one of my favorite patients, a middle-aged lady and dog owner. We always chat about Margo and her dog, "Mookie." She also had some puppies recently, and offered us one, by text message :)

The sad—Monica Potts gave her three months notice at Malcolm X. She is resigning.

I knew she was struggling, but it took me as a bit of a surprise, and it's a bummer. She's my closest friend at the health center, and a big-time union organizer. But something tipped her over the edge. She told me it was MEGA and the 15-minute visits, the hamster wheel. But I know Gaza contributed, and she is open about her mental health struggles. Too much stress :(

The question is how can I support my friend; and, how do I respond? I thought about organizing the white coat walkout next week—we can't afford to lose another good primary care doctor. Monica's patients can't afford to lose her. They really can't.

But I might be kissing my medical license goodbye—I think the Physician Help Inc clinical skills assessment will be happening very soon.

Yours, Phil

November 11, Saturday 6:48 AM
Dearest Al,

Australia!

Last night our friend Raj came over for dinner—he used to live in Beacon Hill with his wife and family but moved to Melbourne, where she is from. He painted a rosy picture of "Down Under"—particularly, no guns; a much more functional health care system than America's (no insurance companies or billing); and, a solid social safety net. He thinks I could get a medical license there, even with my history. So why don't we move to Australia, particularly with the 2024 Presidential election looming?

The main reason: my mom (and also Wayharmoni, in Los Angeles). Australia is so far, far away—we'd have to take my mother with us.

Of course, other reasons include Joe's school/friends; Margo; and our lives here in Boston.

But a fresh start in Melbourne—boy, is that appealing. Better than Seoul, Minneapolis, Tijuana, etc. Any downsides? Fires in Victoria (the climate is similar to California's); and Rupert Murdoch, founder of Fox News, is from there. Still, Raj says the right wing in Australia is much weaker than here.

There's a sense of social cohesion in Victoria, he reported; support for the marginalized. Melbourne—a land of milk and

honey. We should at least go visit.
Yours, Phil

November 12, Sunday 8:30 AM
Dearest Al,
I'm in Manchester, New Hampshire—the race starts in a few minutes. Marathon mindset! 26.2 miles, I can do it.
Yours, Phil

November 13, Monday 6:26 AM
Dearest Al,
The race was awesome. I ran with the 5-hour pacers, a couple of folks from Natick, the entire way. And I had the energy for a strong "kick" at the end—so as I sprinted toward the finish line I had my arms up and was smiling and gesturing to the crowd—they cheered in response! 4 hours, 59 minutes, 38 seconds! About 20 minutes better than my previous best, Providence!
So I learned a lot, from these 4 marathons, about preparation, including focusing on the details. I don't even have any toe blisters or cuts, because I trimmed my nails before the race and applied copious vaseline.
Most importantly, I drove home safely from Manchester to Boston, even though I was exhausted. Survival = success.
Yours, Phil

November 14, Tuesday 4:36 AM
Dearest Al,
I had a pretty bad experience at my new primary care physician's office yesterday. It was like the actor William Hurt in the 1991 movie, "The Doctor."
I went for one reason—to get a silly form filled out for

Malcolm X Health Center, an "Annual Communicable Disease and Immunization Screening form," so I can maintain my credentialing. Yes, I had a Tdap in the last ten years. Yes, I had a negative PPD in the past year (which isn't even required by CDC guidelines anymore). Yes, I had a flu shot.

Anyway, the visit started with the doctor not introducing herself. Then she jumped into a bunch of questions, machine gun style.

"Do you drink?"

"Do you smoke?"

"Do you vape?"

"Do you wear seatbelts?"

"Do you have a gun in the home"

"Have you ever done IV drugs?"

"Are you sexually active?"

Etc.

I got nervous during the barrage of questions, and my blood pressure was a little high (white coat hypertension, almost certainly, because at home before the visit it was 120/77). So my PCP repeated my blood pressure twice, then told me she was going to do an EKG. That was mildly abnormal, with an RSR' in lead V1, the computer "suggesting right ventricular conduction delay." And I got pretty scared I was going to drop dead, even though I ran a marathon the day before.

The visit ended with her ordering me to go down to the laboratory for blood and urine tests. Instead, I ran out the side door and there's no way in hell I'm going back to that clinic.

Yours, Phil

November 15, Wednesday 5:26 AM

Dearest Al,

Well, I'm still alive :) Despite my EKG, with its right ventricular conduction delay / partial right bundle branch block. I tossed and turned last night, but I don't think it was so much because of fear of sudden cardiac death. Rather, it's MEGA, and the primary care treadmill!

I have eleven patents scheduled between 8 AM—12:30 PM today, and then ten more tomorrow between 5—8 PM.

I'd almost say Malcolm X management is trying to drive me to quit, like they did (I believe) to Dr. Monica Potts, because she's a union organizer. But I'm not that cynical about our health center leadership. Medicine in America is a big business, and we are $4.5 million in the red (projections from Naren).

But no matter. I've got my marathon mindset and some new self-confidence after the awesome experience in New Hampshire over the weekend. I just need to find my "pacers" (i.e. fellow health care workers) to support me as we see these patients, organize, and vote "Yes" for the union!

Life is a marathon.

Yours, Phil

November 16, Thursday 5:26 AM

Dearest Al,

Yesterday I saw a patient with occupational asthma, an undocumented lady who works in a sweatshop / factory just outside Boston. Her kids are back in her home country; here, she lives with roommates. I tried to refer her to an immigration lawyer, but I'm not optimistic.

Probably her best shot to get paperwork would be to marry a U.S. citizen.

Yours, Phil

November 17, Friday 5:30 AM

Dearest Al,

My cell phone rang—it was Monica Potts.

"Phil, you've got to get out here. Your patient has a knife," she exclaimed tightly.

And it was true. Although the patient had put it away by the time I arrived, there she paced, agitated, wide eyed, in the middle of the waiting room.

"I'm here for Dr. Philip," she told the receptionist.

We called the police. Six officers came and surrounded her.

I filled out the Section 12 paperwork—application for an authorization of temporary involuntary hospitalization. And EMS arrived and took her away.

I still had more patients to see—a man with mysterious burning abdominal pain; a woman with hypertriglyceridemia and a recent gallbladder removal.

At Malcolm X Health Center, we need metal detectors, so people don't bring knives and guns into our clinic.

Yours, Phil

November 18, Saturday 6:36 AM

Dearest Al,

I'm sitting with John at the breakfast table, and he's diagramming football plays.

"Of course the tight end goes over the middle," he says.

I try to be Zen, to focus on the moment, to forget about yesterday at Malcolm X. Dr. Duva announced Monica Potts departure, almost gleefully, during an all-staff meeting. Mon sat next to Therese, who was shaking with rage, at management's hardhanded behavior.

After an urgent care clinic session, I was summoned to an

emergency debriefing regarding the knife incident. Management refused to get metal detectors for the health center entrances. Instead, they want to "Reeducate" us about how to call a code silver, active shooter...

So I wrote a petition—a safe working environment at Malcolm X; and keep Dr. Monica Potts. We'll sleep on it for a couple of days, and perhaps start signing on Monday.

Meanwhile, I think we need a "Hail Mary" in the union election—but maybe we just need to grind it out, vote by vote.

We need to win—one of the Malcolm X MBA administrators callously said the knife patient will be coming back to see me once she gets out of the Section 12 psych hold.

Yours, Phil

November 19, Sunday, 6:40 AM

Dearest Al,

Six weeks left to cross the abyss. Six weeks until New Year's Eve. I will finish this DDD book, and my CD, and do my best to help us win the union election. I will focus on my goals, stay zennish, and follow my plan. It's as if I'm at mile 25 of a marathon, legs burning, chest tight, but I'm holding on to "kick" at the sight of the finish line.

But today—Sunday—this is one more weekend day for family and for rest. I'm off to Planet Fitness to do some weightlifting. Later on Joe has swimming, then soccer. And Oma announced she is going back to her Korean church, after a long absence (basically the entire pandemic).

So we keep improvising, and we give thanks as Thanksgiving approaches.

Thanks for this home, this warmth.

Tomorrow at 4 PM I'm going to the Massachusetts State

House for a candlelight vigil in support of homeless families and children across the Commonwealth. The organizer asked me to say a few words—so I plan to talk about my patients who have unstable housing, and the link to poor health outcomes—diabetes, mental health, substance use disorder, HIV, etc.

Never give up.

Yours, Phil

November 20, Monday, 5:17 AM

Dearest Al,

Another week is here, and yesterday was good. We had John's swim lesson in Brookline, then Oma drove to Medford while John and I rode the Green and Orange lines home. Nine years old—you blink, and look how big your child has become. How intelligent, how mature (most of the time).

In the afternoon we had his last soccer game of the season at English High School, and then we went over to the Vargas' house for dinner. Balazs is originally from Hungary, and his wife Sally made cold fruit soup along with vegetarian lasagna. Before dinner, Wilfredo and John played a balloon game which was similar to capture the flag.

Good times. Before COVID we might not have appreciated an indoor dinner with friends so much.

Speaking of gratitude, a friend of mine, a soccer league organizer and man who is paraplegic because of an accident invited me to a dinner being held for Haitian refugees here in Boston. So the vigil is today, and the dinner is tomorrow. A busy week.

One step at a time. Don't run your race alone. Preparation. Visualization. And neuroplasticity! Yes, our brains can change for the positive, with focus and deliberate effort. Pace yourself.

Yours, Phil

November 21, Tuesday, 5:23 AM

Dearest Al,

So yesterday I found myself back at the State House for the candlelight vigil in support of the homeless families and children. Migrants have it so difficult in this country—and the governor, legislature, and all of us, are not doing nearly enough.

They did give me the microphone, and I said a few words about housing, human rights and health.

Then, when I got home, my "Official Secret Ballot" from the National Labor Relations Board had arrived. I put on my SEIU 1199 purple tee-shirt and took a selfie—then texted the photo around.

I also signed up for my 5th marathon—Jekyll Island, Georgia, on January 14th. Ron is also running the race. I got a plane ticket and Motel 6 room, and just need a rental car.

Today—I have a visit with Dr. Roy G. Basch, my psychiatrist, over at Man's Greatest Hospital. I'm going to see if he would be willing to write a letter urging Malcolm X to install metal detectors as a "reasonable accommodation" under the Americans with Disabilities Act. Preserving a safe workplace = promoting physical and mental health.

And last night John and I played soccer for an hour in the living room, while Oma was at Zumba at Curtis Hall. Life is good.

Yours, Phil

November 22, Wednesday, 5:24 AM

Dearest Al,

Onward. Dr. Roy G. Basch agreed to email Naren requesting Malcolm X Health Center install metal detectors (one of his

Man's Greatest Hospital psychiatry colleagues was stabbed in 2009 by a patient with bipolar).

Later, I worked on MEGA, trying to finish my notes—the game of Whac-A-Mole continues. I also chatted with Monica Potts—she is doing much better, but told me to beware of Dr. Duva—"a wolf in sheep's clothing." She seemed reluctant to have me circulate the petition on her behalf. It would put a target on my back, even more than it already is, as a union supporter.

Keep my head down—especially because Doctor Evaluation Inc and Physician Help Inc are closing in on me for the skills assessment. They want access to MEGA to review my charts, by December 1st—they're like vultures circling.

In the evening, I went to the event in Hyde Park with the Haitian refugees. Even though they are quasi-homeless, there was much singing, dancing, and merriment.

Yours, Phil

November 23, Thursday, 7:27 AM

Dearest Al,

Thanksgiving. I stayed up late watching the 1991 William Hurt movie, "The Doctor." In it, he gets diagnosed with laryngeal cancer and wakes up to the importance of empathy, of humanism in medicine. And this was an era in which computers were barely used, when MEGA hadn't even been invented.

Yesterday it rained heavily, and primary care clinic was a bit slower, and fun in some ways. I saw a couple I'd known since I started at Malcolm X—they brought their poodle to the health center. It was white, and had its paws and ears dyed green.

And this book is winding down. I'll write tomorrow, Saturday, and Sunday, then send the manuscript in to BCP Digital Printing. Hopefully, I'll also record the CD this weekend with Ben Benson.

Yours, Phil

November 24, Friday, 5:42 AM
Dearest Al,
I just had some post-Thanksgiving seitan—remember one year ago—chewy as steak...
We had a nice day yesterday. John and I ran his first 5K ever, at Jamaica Pond. He went out very fast, sprinting with his friend Mack Mickelson—but they slowed down, and the three of us stayed together the whole way. They broke 31 minutes—impressive for eight/nine year olds.
Then, I listened to a live webcast from Plymouth, Massachusetts, the National Day of Mourning, put on by a Native American group. How can we protect the land; connect with our ancestors; keep fighting for peace, in this violent world?
Later, my mom came over for the meal with her sister, who had driven up from Toledo, Ohio. It was very nice; Kathy (and John) did a tremendous job preparing everything. I'm grateful.
So here we are—Thanksgiving one year, so many things happen, then Thanksgiving the next year. It makes me think of Marcel Proust—Remembrance of Things Past—Swann's Way. You read Proust, along with many other books, when you were in prison, a half-century ago. Shawshank.
We can escape the prisons that enclose us.
Yours, Phil

November 25, Saturday, 6:37 AM
Dearest Al,
I want to write about my own racism.
I recently saw an African-American male patient, about 24-years-old. He came late to his appointment, wore a big puffy

jacket, slumped in the exam room chair. It was the first time I was meeting him, and I logged into MEGA. There was a scanned discharge summary—he had recently been admitted to a psychiatric hospital for some odd behaviors.

After the knife patient recently, I was on edge, as this young man spoke about the "misunderstanding" which had gotten him into the locked ward. I didn't feel threatened, per se, but I was far from the exam room door if he were to pull out a weapon.

But I kept asking him questions, and he soon told me the name of the top schools he had attended; his college major; the courses he had most enjoyed; and his prior jobs.

I was filled with shame. He wasn't a threat to me. Sure, he was depressed, but he spoke cogently. Openly.

We hold powerful, dangerous stereotypes—of young, black men; of people with mental illness.

Yours, Phil

November 26, Sunday, 7:00 AM

Dearest Al,

Well, this book is done. I'm sitting on the couch next to Margo... she's licking and scratching herself. The radiators are hissing, and I see the sunrise out past our new Christmas tree.

I remove her Rabbitgoo harness and she stops scratching, but continues licking.

I had a good meditation just now... loving kindness. Breathe.

Yesterday we listened to the Ohio State-Michigan game on the radio (internet)—we lost, but it was close. Then, we went to Grandma's—my aunt was still there, and we ate my mom's raisin bread as John drew.

We talked about Nanna, the house on Rockingham, the barn in back, the old times. Rosary Cathedral, the Catholic funerals with clanging incense, Grandpa Pete's poodles, his hobbies of painting and gardening. Nanna's love for the Detroit Tigers. Which siblings shared bedrooms with whom.

And we spoke about the next generation, John; and my aunt's kids and grandchildren.

Margo is still licking herself, over and over. I hear birds outside; John's voice in the other room.

Thanks, Dad.

Yours, Phil

About the Author

Philip A. Lederer was born in Columbus, Ohio in 1980 and graduated from the University of Pennsylvania School of Medicine. He lives with his family in Jamaica Plain, Massachusetts.

You can connect with me on:
🌐 http://www.philiplederer.net